C000130033

Wedding at the Castle of Dreams

by
S J Crabb

2

Copyrighted Material

Copyright © S J Crabb 2020

S J Crabb has asserted her rights under the
Copyright, Designs and Patents Act 1988 to be
identified as the Author of this work.

This book is a work of fiction and except in the
case of historical fact, any resemblance to actual
persons, living or dead, is purely coincidental.

All rights reserved. No part of this book may be
reproduced or transmitted in any form without
written permission of the author, except by a
reviewer who may quote brief passages for review
purposes only.

NB: This book uses UK spelling.

Contents

Romantic Comedy

More books by S J Crabb

The Diary of Madison Brown

My Perfect Life at Cornish Cottage

My Christmas Boyfriend

Jetsetters

More from Life

A Special Kind of Advent

Fooling in love

Will You

Holly Island

Aunt Daisy's Letter

The Wedding at the Castle of Dreams

sjcrabb.com

The perfect wedding, or so she thought.
The fairy-tale castle was the perfect setting.
The venue couldn't be any more romantic and the man she was set to marry was straight out of the book of Happy ever after.

The scene was set and nothing was left to chance; it was perfect in every way.

Then the guests arrived and Lily discovered they hadn't read the memo.

Unwelcome guests, parents on the edge of insanity and friends who think they know best make this a wedding Lily wishes was over already.

A legend that dooms the marriage before it's even begun and a happily ever after that may not make it past the speeches.

Lily is about to discover there is no such thing as the perfect day and you can't plan for the unexpected.

The Wedding at the Castle of Dreams follows Lily and Finn's story from Aunt Daisy's Letter. You do not have to read it to enjoy this story & if you enjoy this can go back and see how it all began.

It's how it ends that's undecided!

♥ 1

"Once upon a time."

"Really mum, I'm not five you know."

"I wish you were sometimes; you certainly act like it."

Sighing heavily, I sink back on the bed and try to fight my frustration. They've only just arrived and my family are irritating me.

"Are you ok, Lily, love?"

My nan's anxious face peers at me from the seat by the window because she needs an upright chair and she wouldn't be able to get out of this bed if she got in. She's accustomed to the orthopaedic one that appears to place her in a standing position and wash and dress her at the same time.

"I'm fine, just a little anxious." I try to smile but it's getting increasingly harder to relax because my 'to do' list is growing by the hour, reminding me I'm not as organised as I think I am.

She looks concerned as mum rolls her eyes. "Which is precisely why I volunteered my story telling services. Now, where was I?"

My friend Heidi nudges me and grins and I try to stem the slightly hysterical giggle that is threatening to send my mother over the edge.

As slumber parties go, this one is a little unusual. I am surrounded by my nearest and dearest who arrived earlier today for my wedding in the Chateau de Rêves, or in English, The Castle of Dreams. It's where I live with my fiancé and have done for the past two years. We are converting it to a super luxury retreat and to say the progress is slow is an understatement.

Despite everything, I love it so hard it hurts. What was once a crumbling ruin on the verge of extinction, is now a potential Castle of Dreams as its name suggests. Finn and I love the place equally and gave up everything to see the dream reinstated from the nightmare it became. Yes, The Castle of Nightmares is its adopted new name, but I know it's there. The romance is buried under the builder's dust and the cobwebs of several generations of spiders. The drafty windows look over an amazing landscape that promises so much and delivers even more. The four turrets that stand proudly guarding the castle secrets are majestic and indicative of a time when life was very different and the huge open fireplaces in every room burn with a warmth that brings the life back to a forgotten paradise.

Once upon a time is not that far off the mark because I imagine this place was a fairy-tale castle when it was built and now mum has got a story to tell about something she discovered on google.

I am looking forward to hearing her story despite my interruption and look across with interest as she makes herself comfortable in the chair next to nan and smiles mysteriously.

"As I was saying before I was so rudely interrupted…" She glares at me and I shrink a little in my seat as I revert back to that five-year-old girl who couldn't get away with anything around her.

"Once upon a time in a land far away and forgotten, stood a majestic castle. It was the jewel in the crown of a man who longed for the finer things in life. He had great wealth and used the castle to store it all. Word soon spread and people came from far and wide to catch a glimpse of a castle that was rumoured to be clad in gold bars. However, inside this castle of great wealth was a lonely man. He had everything that his money could buy but one thing – love. He had nobody to share his passion with except for his servants, and he became bitter and jealous of other people's happiness. Soon, he became consumed with a thirst for finding the last piece of a puzzle he was anxious to finish and decreed that he would hold a ball in this very castle to find the woman he would marry."

"Oh, I've heard this one already."

We look at nan in surprise as she shrugs. "Cinderella; it's obvious. Honestly, Sonia, I'm surprised by your lack of originality."

I smirk as mum bristles with indignation. "This is not Cinderella, far from it. You know, you've always been the same, interrupting without knowing the facts first. Now, if you will just let me finish, you will see that this is definitely *not* Cinderella, or even remotely like it."

Nan rolls her eyes making Heidi and me giggle and mum sighs. "Do you want to hear the story or not?"

9

"I do."

Heidi's hand shoots up and I snort. "We're not in class, you know. What's with the hand?"

"Just demonstrating my eagerness for a good old-fashioned tale."

She grins and I can't help but join her. Heidi always did make me laugh, which is why we are such good friends. It was lucky she could make the wedding at all because lately she always appears to be travelling with her boyfriend Thomas who she met under very romantic circumstances at a Ball we attended when she was actually dressed as Cinderella. You just couldn't make it up!

Mum says crossly, "Anyway, no more interruptions, you're disturbing my flow."

"I can't remember what a flow is. I need to go so often only a trickle comes out every time."

Nan looks at us sadly. "Don't get old dears, your body is way ahead of your mind and it's quite a surprise when you realise you're not that young woman with the world at her feet anymore. All you are left with is a battered body that is failing on every level and a mind that still wants what it once had."

Mum reaches across and squeezes her hand gently. "Don't worry, Sandra, you're in the Castle of Dreams now and who knows what will happen? Anyway, let me finish because I will need a cup of tea soon and the thought of walking down the millions of steps to get it is not a happy one. You know, Lily, you really should consider tea and

10

coffee making facilities in every room - just saying."

Taking a deep breath, she carries on.

"There was great excitement, as you can imagine. Word spread far and wide and it was all anyone could speak of. Every young girl in the land was hopeful of marrying the rich and handsome young man. The older women just wanted a peek inside a virtual palace and the men were interested in mixing with the many young ladies on offer. Yes, it was the gathering of the century and as you can imagine, no expense was too great for the wealthy young man. The day soon dawned and it was a glorious one. The sun beat down on a day filled with preparation and excitement. By the time the evening came, the castle was transformed into a fairy tale palace with food, drink and music bursting from every room and window. The people came and it was a splendid sight and they were met by the wealthy man who owned the castle. One by one, the women were presented to him, but they didn't appear to measure up. Something was missing until one in particular caught his eye. A beautiful girl in a white dress appeared and curtsied low before him. Flowers were woven into her hair that hung long down her back and the eyes that raised to his were as blue as cornflowers and sparkled with happiness. He caught his breath because this girl was as pure as the driven snow and appeared untouched by human hand. She could

11

be an angel and from the moment her eyes met his, he knew she was the one. He couldn't look away and reaching out, took her hand to help her to her feet as she bowed before him, and led her to the dance floor. As his arm encircled her waist, he resisted the urge to ask everyone to leave because he knew he had found the greatest treasure. As he spun her around the dance floor, he was so happy he thought his heart would burst."

"What were their names?"

"What?"

Mum looks irritated as nan says loudly, "Their names. It's all very well telling us about the wealthy handsome young man and the beautiful girl, but quite frankly, they could have terrible names. What were they?"

"I don't know."

"What do you mean, you're telling the story? Didn't you google them?"

"If I did, it didn't mention names, none I can remember, anyway. What difference does it make?"

"A lot. I mean, I can't picture them unless they have a name."

"I know."

We turn and look at Heidi as she says with excitement, "Call them Finn and Lily. That would be so romantic and quite fitting considering why we're here."

"Oh, I don't think that's a good idea."

Mum looks worried and nan smiles brightly. "Of course, I'm with Heidi on this. Yes, Finn and Lily are the heroes of this story, carry on."

"No, I don't think…"

"For goodness' sake, Sonia, I'm the edge of needing another wee and won't make it back if I have to leave. Finish your story and then put me out of my misery."

I flash mum a warning not to upset nan and she shrugs and carries on.

"He never left her side all night. To say he was intoxicated with desire is an understatement. She was everything he was looking for and he couldn't see past his own desire to have her."

"Now you're talking."

"Sandra, for goodness' sake."

"What, this is the good bit, carry on Sonia."

Nan winks at me and I laugh softly as mum says wearily, *"He led her to a hidden staircase and promised to show her his greatest treasure."*

This time we all burst out laughing and mum shouts, "Enough with the childish behaviour, I'm getting to the good bit."

"You can say that again." Nan grins and trying hard to stifle our laughter, we practice restraint as mum leans forward and lowers her voice.

13

"He led um... Lily away from the party into the topmost turret where he stored his most valuable possessions and she had never seen such riches. She was blown away by um... Finn's wealth and intoxicated on greed. He promised her his entire kingdom if she would be his bride and as he asked her to become his wife, she answered with words he didn't want to hear. 'No.'

He couldn't believe it. He was offering her the world and she said no. He became enraged and demanded why and she told him fearfully that she was betrothed to another. A man that was cruel and vicious and the man nobody wanted to meet because he was known to kill a man just for the pleasure of hearing him scream. Her parents had arranged the marriage and they were set to marry two weeks from the day. The only reason she came was to take one last lingering look at freedom before he locked her away forever. Well, Finn was enraged. He was so angry that his beloved Lily was betrothed to a beast and vowed he would do everything in his power to save her. She was frightened and begged him to let her go because the man..."

"Bert."

"No, Sandra, we are not calling the evil man Bert."

Heidi giggles as nan shrugs. "Why not, it amuses me?"

"Nan, you can't liken grandad to a beast of a man who kills for pleasure. It's not right."

14

"Why not, it's just for fun?"

Mum shakes her head and says wearily, *"um, Bert would want revenge and they wouldn't be safe. However, Finn couldn't see past his own desire to own such a treasure and flew into a rage. He wouldn't take no for an answer and locked Lily in the tower so she couldn't escape. He made everyone leave and nobody knew what he had done. He thought no one would ever know and for the next two weeks she was his prisoner, only taking her food, water and washing facilities, while telling her he was keeping her safe from a madman.*

Well, two weeks to the day, he was paid an unwelcome visit. Bert had discovered where Lily was and wanted his property back. It was his wedding day and he was in no mood to hang around, so with a huge army of men, he stormed the Castle of Dreams and left no stone unturned in his quest to find her. Finn was no match for the evil Bert and was cut down on the spot. His head was sliced cleanly off and Bert was rumoured to have grabbed it by the hair and carried it with him to find his errant bride. It didn't take long and he soon 'rescued' her from the tower and presented her with the head of her erstwhile captor. Lily was overcome with grief and fear. She saw the madness in Bert's eyes as he prepared to take what was his, and so she did the only thing she could think of. She jumped from the window and fell to her death below. Bert's roar of rage was heard throughout

*the land and as he held the head of the man who
had taken his bride, he cursed the Castle of Dreams
and vowed that no living soul would ever find
happiness inside these walls. Then he plundered
Finn's wealth and murdered his staff and retreated
back to his own palace of destruction. Legend has it
that his curse remains to this day and only true
love's kiss will break it. When the curse lifts, it will
reveal the location of the greatest treasure that
remains hidden – the treasure of the Castle of
Dreams that was never found and is thought to be
buried somewhere nearby, waiting for the light of
day to restore this place to its previous splendour."*

There's a stunned silence as she finishes and
then nan says, "Typical Bert."

We stare at her in amazement as she shrugs.
"Probably some ancestor he forgot to tell me
about."

"Never mind grandad, what on earth possessed
you to tell that tale a week before my wedding?
Honestly mum, even for you this is a new low."

Mum shrugs. "It's only a story, ok, a legend, but
it was years ago. As if things like that happen now."

"According to you they do, all the time as it
happens." Mum has an unhealthy obsession with
murder most foul and this is right up her street.

Heidi interrupts, "I can see why you were
reluctant to use Lily and Finn, hardly happy ever
after, was it?"

We stare at each other gloomily and then mum says brightly, "Anyway, who fancies that cup of tea? I brought some digestives because I wasn't sure if they did them in France. Come on Sandra, we can stop off for a comfort break on the way."

As they leave, Heidi throws me a sympathetic look and squeezes my arm. "Fairy tales were always so grim, weren't they? Thank goodness the world became civilised and things like that would have serious repercussions these days. Maybe it's best to look forward, not back. Now, I've got a bottle of gin in my room, do you fancy a sundowner?"

As I follow Heidi to her room, I try to push down any unease my mother's story caused. Rubbish. Complete and utter rubbish and I will absolutely never think of that story again as long as I live.

"I can't stop thinking about that stupid story."

Finn groans and turns to face me. "It's only a story, Adams, don't let it get to you."

"Easy for you to say, you have the ability to switch off from the cold hard facts of life. I don't have that luxury because I'm sensitive."

Grinning, he reaches across and pulls me close and then starts tickling me mercilessly.

Shrieking, I try to get away but it's an impossible task because he is way stronger than me and used to disarming his adversaries. I almost can't breathe as the tears run down my face as I squirm in his arms and giggle so loudly, they must hear me back in England.

Thankfully, he stops and replaces it with a sweet and loving kiss that I much prefer. In fact, I could kiss him all day long because he is that good and I am still pinching myself that he came into my life at all.

After a while, he stops and looks into my eyes and says gently, "Better?"

"I'm not sure."

"Why?"

"I may need some more reassurance."

His eyes sparkle and he needs no further invitation and then we hear a terse voice outside the door, "For goodness' sake, Lily, is there any hot water in this place, my shower's freezing?"

Finn groans as I leap from the bed and grab my dressing gown, feeling as if I've been caught in a compromising position by my mother as I revert back to a teenager again. Finn starts to laugh as I hop on one foot as I try to slip my foot into the rather fetching slipper sock that Heidi knitted for me and shout, "I'm just coming."

"Chance would be a fine thing."

"Stop it Finn, she'll hear you." I glare at him and he turns and groans, pulling the pillow over his head as I stumble to the door and on opening it, see my mum looking cross, dressed only in a towel and shivering with cold.

"Mum, go and get some clothes on, you'll freeze."

"I wouldn't if there was any hot water in this place. You know, Lily, you really should get that sorted. I mean, no five-star luxury resort should be without it. Just think of the bad reviews you'll get on Trip Advisor. After all, the paying public are not as forgiving as I am. They won't hold back you know and could ruin your business before it's even started, then where will you be?"

I try to tune her out, but it's impossible as she follows me downstairs. "Imagine if it was your nan, it could have sent her to an early grave."

"What are you talking about?" I feel frustrated that she interrupted an illicit moment of pleasure and she says sharply, "The icy shock could have stopped her heart in an instant and then you would forever have her murder on your conscience."

19

"Seriously, I doubt anyone's ever been murdered by a shower, don't be so melodramatic."

"Of course they have, haven't you heard of Bates motel?"

"This isn't Pyscho and I'm not Norman Bates, yet, anyway."

Grabbing a torch from the drawer in the kitchen, I head to the boiler cupboard behind the utility room and mum says irritably, "I feel like a psycho most days to be honest. It's not easy you know, dealing with your father."

"What are you talking about?"

I shine the torch in the cupboard, reminding myself to get light installed in here as quickly as possible, as mum grumbles, "A retired man is a lazy one, Lily. Ever since he hung up his briefcase, he's been getting under my feet. I can't turn around without almost falling over him and the house is never tidy. He's always leaving his mess around and expecting me to pick it up. It's no wonder I get up early just to get a little distance from him. I'm telling you, darling, Norman Bates will have nothing on me if he doesn't find a hobby or part-time job soon."

Despite myself I start to laugh picturing my mother as Norman Bates and she says irritably, "It's no joke. The man is seriously getting on my nerves and I may have to resort to desperate measures."

"Which are?"

Flicking on the switch that has tripped again, I decide to get Finn to take a look when he actually decides to leave the comfort of his bed and mum says, "He will have to come here and help you. Maybe you can employ him as a handyman, or a gardener, anything really just to give me five minutes peace, what do you say, shall I tell him it's all arranged?"

"No mum, you will do no such thing. Long distance romances are doomed to fail and if dad was here in France, you would be lonely."

"Chance would be a fine thing."

"Why don't you find him some jobs to do around the house? I'm guessing after a week of being ordered around he'll find something to occupy him, sharpish."

"Maybe. You know you're right, Lily. I should be more creative with my problem and think of a cunning plan to get him out of my hair. Thanks darling, I knew I could count on you to see my side."

"I'm not taking sides; I'm doing it for both your sanities."

Turning to face her, I smile with relief. "There, give it a minute and it should heat up. Do you fancy a cup of tea while you wait?"

"That sounds good, although I wouldn't need one if I had tea and coffee making facilities in my room, as well as a working tv. You really should shape up, darling, I don't think you've thought this through at all."

Taking a deep breath, I say in a measured voice, "I told you a million times already, all of that is on

21

order and will be in place for the paying guests." I stare at her pointedly and she shrugs. "A little late if I'm honest. This was your perfect opportunity to test out your hospitality. After all, how many guests are you expecting this week?"

I start to tick them off on my fingers. "Well, there's you and dad of course and nan and grandad. Finn's parents arrive today along with his nan and grandpa. Sable and Arthur will be arriving in two days' time and so will Heidi's boyfriend Thomas. Mark said he should be here within the next two days, along with his plus one."

Mum looks excited and the tears well up in her eyes. "I can't wait. You know, skype is no substitute for holding my baby in my arms."

For a moment I feel the emotion threaten to choke me as I see the love in my mum's eyes for her baby boy, my brother Mark, who semi-emigrated to Australia nearly three years ago. I think mum saw him once, six months after he left when her and dad took a holiday down under. He's been moving around ever since and is now finally heading home to take responsibility for his life and he is not coming alone.

"What's her name?"

"Kylie, I think?"

"Seriously?"

Mum nods. "It's a popular name out there. Who knows, it may actually be *the* Kylie, she would be lucky, lucky, lucky, if it was, Mark is quite a catch."

I grin as I picture my brother without a mother's rose-tinted spectacles on and just remember a rather lazy, scruffy introvert, who hardly said two words and just grunted his response every time anyone asked him a question. It's the same when I call him and I'm intrigued to see how he managed to actually ask a girl out in the first place, let alone get her to join him on a long flight to meet his family. This should be interesting.

"Are Finn's parents still fighting?"

Shaking myself, I look up and sigh. "Apparently so. I just hope they leave that behind and behave themselves this week, for their son's sake."

The kettle boils and as I fill the mugs, I think about Finn's parents. Stella and Piers Roberts. Poles apart in every way and yet still married and fast approaching their pearl wedding. Every time I see them, they have a disagreement and I can see now why Finn joined the special forces. Anything to get away from the war inside their home as they tear strips off each other and plot counter attacks as they would their daily menu. Despite it all, I have a very soft spot for his father because he is good fun and despite having a wandering eye, is always funny and entertaining. Stella is an amazing woman, which makes it even worse that Piers has lost interest in her, resulting in some terrible arguments.

Sighing, I sit at the kitchen table and say sadly, "I just hope they behave for Finn's sake. He's dreading this week because they are coming."

"They're still his parents, Lily. He should be looking forward to seeing them."

"Oh he is, I mean, individually. You know, they've even asked for separate bedrooms, that's not right, is it mum?"

She sips her tea, looking thoughtful. "I wonder why? Actually, I feel a little annoyed I didn't think of that. Just think, my own space away from your father hogging the bed sheets and snoring all night. You know, I woke up the other night and thought we were being attacked, his snoring resembled machine gun fire and I almost rolled under the bed in fright."

I start to laugh and she says crossly, "It's ok for you, you're still in the flush of love, I'm guessing Finn can do nothing wrong in your eyes. Well, let me tell you young lady, that feeling soon passes when you can't sleep through the night anymore and the lines merge with the bags under your eyes and you age overnight."

Picturing Finn waiting for me upstairs, I get a warm feeling inside. I certainly hit the jackpot with him and can't wait to marry him. We have an amazing life here in France at the Castle of Dreams and I'm looking forward to starting our family as soon as the ink has dried on our wedding certificate. Yes, a little Finn or Lily is definitely on the cards and this is the perfect place to raise them in.

Feeling in a better mood as I picture my perfect family, I say brightly, "Anyway, the water should be hot now. I'll leave you to it and go and get ready.

Don't forget we won't be able to linger over breakfast because we're heading into town to pick up my wedding dress before the others arrive."

Mum looks excited. "I can't wait, darling. You know, it's every mother's dream to see her little girl in her wedding dress. I just wish I'd been here when you chose it."

Feeling a little bad, I smile and say softly, "I'm sorry, mum. It was a spur-of-the-moment decision and as it was on sale at the time, I didn't have long. I just hope they managed to alter it. I mean, it may have been tricky to let out the waist as much as they needed to and it was a little long but they're professionals and know what they're doing. I'm sure it's perfectly lovely."

Mum looks at me sharply. "What do you mean, let out the waist? Are you piling on the pounds gorging on French patisserie every day because if you are, it will only end in tears you know?"

"Of course not. It was just a few sizes too small. I'm still the same size I've been since I was fifteen. The dress I chose was obviously designed with a supermodel in mind because it was a sample from Givenchy's wedding range. I can't begin to tell you how happy I was to find it. As you know, I'm no supermodel but I will feel like one when that silk sensation caresses my skin. Honestly mum, it's a dream come true."

Her face softens and she brushes away a tear. "I can't wait, darling. In fact, I can't wait for it all because it makes me so happy to see you happy. It's all I've ever wanted and now that day is dawning."

She sniffs and then to my surprise reaches out and hugs me. "I'm so proud of you, Lily, I always have been. You have grown into a beautiful young lady and are just the woman I always wanted you to be."

I feel my own eyes filling up and swallowing the sob that's not far away, squeeze her hard. For a moment we cling to each other while the past is replaced by the future. A different relationship will take its place, but I will still need her help to become even half the woman she always was. Yes, I may be planning my own family, but she is an important part of that. My mum will always be the woman I aspire to be and I will look forward to sharing my new life with her beside me every step of the way.

♥*3*

"Are you sure this is the place?"

I stare at the little shop in horror.

It's closed.

In fact, the lights are off and no one's home and I check my watch for the tenth time before peering at the opening hours on the door.

"It should be open, it says 10-4, it's 10.30 now."

Heidi looks through the window and says, "Maybe they've had a lie in."

"Well, we can't stand here loitering all day, is there anywhere we can go for a coffee while we wait?" Nan sounds disgruntled and I feel bad for dragging her here in the first place. It's quite a trek and took us one hour in a car that was minus its air conditioning because it packed up last Thursday and we haven't had the time to get it fixed.

"I think there's a place across the square."

Mum looks around and says firmly, "Then we will go and grab a lovely café au lait and wait. You know, I heard the continentals aren't as rigid in their opening hours as the Brits. I never believed it but now I'm not so sure."

"Honestly mum, stop judging the French, they work really hard and you know nothing."

Mum raises her eyes and feeling a little cross, I stomp off towards the nearest café.

Heidi falls into step beside me and says reassuringly, "It's ok, I'm sure they won't be long."

"I hope so because all I can think of is the curse. What if it's started?"

"Hmm, the thought had crossed my mind. You know, last night I had a dream I was that girl falling from the window. Do you think it happened in the room you gave me; I wouldn't be surprised?"

I stare at her in horror and she shrugs, "You never know."

"Oh, I never thought of that. What if it's *my* room? That would be terrible."

"What would be terrible?"

Mum interrupts us and I say with a slight edge to my voice, "Do you think the tower of treasure and death was the one I sleep in, or Heidi?"

"Possibly, there's no way of knowing."

She looks thoughtful and then nan pipes up, "Maybe we should arrange for one of those psychics to visit, or a priest to exonerate the ghost."
"You mean, exorcise."
"Oh no, Lily, my exercising days are over. I mean, I'm all for keeping fit and all, but if I get down on the floor, I'm liable never to get up again. Verity Perkins told me she tried it and did her back in. She ended up flat on it for two weeks and needed drugging up to the eyeballs for the pain, all in the name of strengthening her core, whatever that is?"

Feeling the frustration threatening to ruin my magical day, I say wearily, "Never mind about the legend of the Castle of Dreams, I need some caffeine to drug me up to my eyeballs just to cope with you lot."

Mum shakes her head and fixes me with a disapproving look. "Don't be so unkind, Lily. I never raised you to talk rudely to your elders."

Heidi squeezes my arm sympathetically and flashes me a smile. Thank god for friends because my tension levels are critical right now.

We soon settle in a little café across the square with a good view of the dress shop and order some café au laits and croissants. I will never tire of this café culture France has perfected so well. I love coming here and relaxing in the sunshine before shopping for delicious antiquities for my new favourite toy. Converting the chateau has been the greatest pleasure and I am so happy that Sable and Arthur allowed Finn and I to invest heavily in it. They are equal partners but aren't hands on. Sable is still editor-in-chief of Designer Homes - *on a budget* and Arthur is an architect. It was always their dream, but the reality was very different and they were only too happy to let me and Finn buy our way in and take over the project management side. Sable still has some say in the décor but is usually happy with my choices, so it works well. I have never regretted giving up my power job in London and I know Finn has never looked back after giving up operational duties as a member of the special forces.

Yes, this was always meant to be and now my mum has ruined the fairy tale with a horror story that is weighing heavily on my mind.

Nan groans as she leans back in her seat and fans her face with a menu.

"Why is France so hot?"
Heidi giggles as mum snaps, "Probably something to do with the climate. Honestly Sandra, what a strange thing to say."

"I never could stand the heat you know; it brings my athlete's foot out."

I place my croissant on my plate and push it away. Gross.

Heidi nods. "I had that once, it took ages to go. I could suggest a few home remedies if you like."

Nan looks interested and as they start chatting, I tune out and look for the hundredth time towards the little shop across the street.

Mum shifts closer and says softly, "It will be fine darling. I'm sure, as Heidi said, they are just running late."

Suddenly, a Volkswagen Beetle pulls up outside the shop and I notice a woman getting out with a bunch of keys in her hand, heading towards the shop.

I say quickly, "Listen guys, stay here and finish your coffees. I'm going to check out the shop, I think they're opening up."

Without waiting for their response, I scrape my chair back and sprint across the square, not caring that I look like a madwoman because there is only one thing on my mind that matters right now – my wedding dress.

Before she's even inside, I stop beside her panting and say breathlessly, "Thank God, I'm here to collect my wedding dress."

The woman looks surprised and then a flash of sympathy passes across her face. "I'm sorry mademoiselle but this shop is closed."

"But..."

I stare at the keys and she shrugs. "I am not the owner. I work for the man who owns the building. The shop has gone out of business and everything inside is now being held by the créanciers, um... how you say, creditors?"

"But that can't be right, my dress is paid for and must be inside. I'm a creditor and I want paying in my dress."

I feel the hysteria rising as the woman shakes her head sadly. "I'm sorry, everything is seized. You can fill out a form on the website and add your name to the list. When it is resolved, you will receive compensation."

"But please... it's inside waiting for me. Probably hanging up with my name on it. Nobody would know and you would make me so happy."

The woman's eyes narrow and she says firmly, "Non, I cannot help you mademoiselle. You must do the form."

"What's going on?"

Mum joins me and I say with a tremor to my voice, "The shop's gone out of business. They won't let me have my dress even though I paid for

31

it."

"Leave this to me, Lily, stand aside."

I recognise the no nonsense voice of a mother who will wrestle angry bears for her daughter and feel the relief hit me hard. Thank God she's here.

Turning to the woman, mum says loudly, "Now listen to me young lady, I am not a patient woman and your cooperation will be most appreciated. Now, we are coming inside this shop and leaving with the dress my daughter has paid for. Nobody needs to know and it's in your best interests to stand aside and let us go about our business. If you don't, I will file a complaint with the office of the President of France myself and let me tell you this for nothing, your job is hanging by a thread right now because I am high up in government and will not tolerate this outrage."

The woman folds her arms and faces my mother and my heart sinks as I see the fierce determination on her face. "Non, we have proper procedures for this and I must ask you to leave before I call the police."

"Call them."

Mum folds her arm in a similar way and they stand facing each other like gladiators facing off before a battle to the death.

"If you insist."

The woman reaches for her phone and starts dialling and I say in horror, "Mum, what are you doing? There's no way they will allow this to happen, let's just leave."

"I will not. This is a matter of principle and I will not walk away unless it's with your dress firmly in my hand."

Nan and Heidi appear and nan says loudly, "What's the matter, Sonia, is this woman giving you trouble?"

Mum nods. "You could say that. She won't give us Lily's dress, so I told her to call the police."

Heidi gasps and nan says with excitement. "Wow, this is great. France is such an exciting place. I can't wait to see what happens, it's like a scene from a movie."

Feeling deeply worried and frustrated at the same time, I pull on my mum's arm. "I think we should go, maybe I'll just call the number instead and leave a message."

No, Lily. Your wedding is in five days' time and we have got more to worry about than your dress. It is hanging inside that shop and we are not leaving until we get it."

The woman looks bored and shrugs, "You may as well leave because I am not helping you."

Heidi butts in and says in a much softer voice, "Excuse me, but I'm sorry for all this. My name is Heidi and I have a shop of my own and totally sympathise with your predicament. You see, the trouble is, we really need that dress because my friend here is getting married in a few days' time and there is no hope of a replacement. Surely it wouldn't hurt to let us take a peek and see if it's there waiting. Please, from one woman who believes in fairy tales to another, please grant us this one wish."

The woman looks at Heidi as if she's an alien and Heidi says sadly, "It's the curse of the Chateau de Rêves, you see."

"The what?"

The woman looks amazed and Heidi nods. "My friend is the owner of the Chateau de Rêves and is in fact staging her own wedding there in a few days' time. The curse of the chateau has raised its head and we need to break the spell for Lily to get her happy ever after. Please, be our fairy godmother and let my Lily go to the ball in the designer dress she paid for. Please, you must believe in love, you are French after all, isn't this the land of romance?"

A flash of doubt flickers across the woman's face and she looks as if she's thinking it through. I can see she's torn and yet Heidi's speech apparently touched a nerve because she says softly, "Le Chateau de Rêves, I'm so sorry, mademoiselle."

"Why?" I feel the fear return as she shakes her head sadly. "I have heard the story too and it's not a happy place. It never has been and this is proof. Maybe you should take this as a warning and abandon your plans."

"Absolutely not, what are you talking about?" Mum looks at her angrily and Heidi steps between them and smiles sweetly. "Please, I'm begging you, just one look."

Feeling the weight of several pairs of eyes on her, the woman groans and taking the keys, unlocks the door. "Ok, only one of you can go inside and look. If it's there with your name attached, I will allow it. If not, you will leave, how you say, empty of the hands."

A surge of hope pushes me through the door and I feel my heart beat faster as I look for the dream dress. It must be here. Surely, it's all boxed up and ready to go and as the woman follows me inside, I set to work.

♥ *4*

"Well, that was a total waste of time."

"Don't say anything, mum."

I keep my eyes on the road and an awkward silence fills the car. There was no sign of my dress when I went into the shop and as I looked frantically around, my heart sank when I realised I would have to leave empty-handed.

The rows of dresses mocked me as I fought back the tears because how on earth can a bride get married without a wedding dress?

To make matters worse, when I ventured outside, it was to see my mum arguing with the French police and nan cheering her on with a rendition of God Save the Queen. Heidi was filming the whole fiasco on her iPhone and although she promised, I bet she posts it on Facebook against my wishes.

I don't think we speak for the whole journey back and I fight the tears that threaten to unravel me. This is a disaster. It's the curse, I just know it is, and I blame my mother for that. As soon as she told us the story, things started going wrong. First the hot water and now my wedding dress. Not to mention the money I've lost in paying for it in the first place.

Thinking of the beautiful gown that was the one of my dreams, a little part of me dies inside. It was only a dress, but it was *the* dress. You know, the one I crafted in my imagination and scoured Pinterest for images of. My wedding board is full of similar images and it's doubtful I will ever be able to look at it again without feeling it tearing at my soul.

As soon as we come to a stop in the cobbled yard of the castle, I wrench open the door and without another word, head towards the lake.

I hear my mum shout, "Lily, don't do this, we can work it out."

I turn and stare at her in confusion. "Do what?"

"Throw yourself in the lake, it's really not worth it."

Finn appears at the front door and apparently hears her because he races over and in one move lifts me off my feet and holds me tight, saying with concern, "It's ok, Lily, I've got you, tell me what happened."

Feeling his arms around me is the final straw and I break down subbing as mum comes over shaking her head.

"The dress is lost, Finn. The shop is in the hands of the receivers and now Lily will have to start again."

He looks astonished. "Is there nothing we can do?"

I cling to him like a child hoping he can make it all go away and shake my head and then nan says with excitement, "I think I have the answer."

We look at her in surprise and she smiles secretly. "Come on, Lily, leave it to your old nan. Come with me, darling."

I see the blood drain from my mum's face and before I can ask why, nan takes my hand and says sweetly, "Come to my room, I may just have the answer."

A sinking feeling settles inside me as I follow her inside. This is not looking good.

It takes us a good ten minutes to reach her room and she chatters excitedly all the way. "You know, Lily, sometimes things happen for a reason and this is one of them. Something must have alerted me to this problem because I have the answer to it."

"What is it, it doesn't involve sewing the sheets together, does it?"

I know my nan only too well and The Sound of Music is her favourite film, especially the part where they make the clothes they need from the curtains because she always told us it was like that when she was a child.

I have a horrible feeling this is one of those moments and the look on my mum's face told me I had every reason to be concerned.

As we head into her room, I notice the orderly precision I have always known her for. She is meticulously tidy and there is never anything out of place, a skill I wish had rubbed off on me as I think about the fact I still haven't even made our bed this morning and last night's clothes are still where they fell when Finn and I crashed into our room after a night on wine and drunken romance.

Shivering with the remembered pleasure of a decadent night of passion, I am distracted momentarily but then the full horror of my situation is revealed as she drags out the case and opens it, revealing a slightly yellowed, extremely creased and overly frilly, wedding dress.

"There, darling, this is just like when you were a little girl and loved to try on my wedding dress. You always told me you would marry in it yourself one day and now that day has arrived. We can give it a gentle clean and it will be as good as new. What do you say, darling, go and try it on for size?"

I can't even speak and just hold out my hands in shock as she thrusts the relic from the past into my arms and as I turn away, the tears prick behind my eyes like acid rain because what on earth can I say to this?

I almost can't bear to try it on but know I must and just pray it doesn't fit because that is the last shred of hope I have.

As the dress slips over my head, a waft of stale musk and moth balls makes me cough and I shudder. As the fabric falls around me, I recoil as it scratches my skin and feels stiff and unyielding. There must be a couple of cans of starch in this dress and it's difficult to move.

Looking into the mirror, I see the resignation in my eyes as a dejected creature stares back at me. The dress looks as bad on as off and I choke down my misery as I contemplate how quickly my big day is unravelling.

"Hurry up, darling, I can't wait to see you."

Swallowing the lump in my throat, I head into the room and my heart sinks as I see the joy on my nan's face as the tears spring from her eyes. She appears overcome with emotion and the sight of is a difficult one as every part of me longs to make her happy, even at the expense of my own happiness.

She stumbles towards me and says with emotion, "It's perfect, darling. You're perfect and you have made me the happiest woman alive. Seeing you in my wedding dress is a dream come true. Your Aunt Daisy, God rest her soul, was adamant she would never wear it but you always told me you would never want another. How lucky that I packed it in case; it's as if the god's have made me your fairy godmother."

My tears join hers, but not for the reason she thinks. This is a disaster. How on earth can I marry Finn dressed like a toilet roll holder? I have exactly four days to think of every reason under the sun why I can't wear this dress without breaking my nan in the process. ˙

Suddenly, the door bursts open and I see my mum's shocked face, closely followed by Heidi's who shrieks behind her, "Go away, Finn, you can't see the bride in her wedding dress."

I stare at them in horror as he shouts, "Are you ok, darlin'?"

My voice is high and slightly hysterical as I shout back, "Fine thanks. Um… Finn."

"Yes?"

"I don't suppose you could crack open a bottle of wine. I'm feeling as if I need a drink."

"But it's only 1o clock, it's a bit early isn't it?"

"No, it's an um… celebration."

Nan beams and mum shakes her head as he shouts, sounding a little relieved, "Ok, I'll set it up outside on the terrace. Your dad and grandad are out there, we could just chill for a bit."

His footsteps lead him away and nan beams, "There, problem solved. Now, Sonia, I will need your help to wash this masterpiece and I think there's a slight tear in the train. Help Lily out of it and then we will work like fairies to get this looking like new for the big day."

Mum goes to say something but my expression tells her to keep it in. I don't want to upset my nan and know that mum would do it in a heartbeat if she thought it was helping me in some way. Heidi throws me a sympathetic look and shakes her head, and I fix a frozen grin on my face as I shimmy out of the dress.

Quickly, I head back to the bathroom and grab my clothes and try to think of a way out of this freshly dug hole.

♥ 5

After two glasses of wine, I start to feel as if the pain has dulled a little and the predicament I'm in doesn't seem as bad. Despite everything, it feels good to have my family around me and I look fondly at my grandad as he laughs at something Heidi is saying.

Finn is resting his arm along the back of my chair as my dad explains the intricacies of golf and mum is brooding over something as she stares into her glass of wine as if the answers lie there.

Nan is upstairs wrestling with the dress of doom and for a moment I try to forget why we are here, just concentrating on chilling with the people I love.

The sun is beating down, reminding me that British people appear to gravitate to the sun at the hottest part of the day when our European neighbours retreat. I suppose that's because we don't enjoy a fraction of the heat they do and make the most of it when it's at its best.

With a new resolve, I decide that's exactly what I must do. Make the best of a bad situation and the dress will just be customised to my wishes. In the grand scheme of things, it doesn't matter what I wear because the only thing that matters is marrying the gorgeous man by my side.

Leaning over, I whisper, "I love you."

He looks at me and the love is reflected right back at me through those gorgeous blue eyes and he smiles softly, "Ok, what do you want?"

"Just you."

He leans in and whispers, "That could be arranged."

Feeling the delicious shiver of expectation run through me, I almost forget we have guests until my father says loudly, "We must play together sometimes."

We all stare at him and he smiles. "Golf. Now I've retired I've decided to make it my new hobby."

"Halleluiah." Mum says loudly and raises her glass to him. "At least it will get you out of the house and away from under my feet. Maybe you should practice every day, say from 9am 'til 6pm. I've heard you need to put the hours in if you want to be captain of the golf club."

"Who said anything about being the captain?"

Dad looks at her in surprise as she shrugs. "If you're going to do something, David, you must aim high. Just think of the functions we could attend. I'm pretty sure you get your own parking space as well and as your wife I would be admired from afar as the woman behind the power golfer. Yes, I can see it now. The members would stare at me in awe as I glide through the hallowed doors and congratulate me on keeping you focused. I would be asked to chair committees and arrange fundraisers and I would do so with grace and determination."

"What are you talking about, I've only played one round, they're hardly likely to offer me the captaincy?"

"Don't be so selfish, David. After all these years of sacrifice on my behalf, you can't even give me the one thing I want the most."

Dad looks completely confused and mum whispers, "Peace and quiet. That's all I want, him out of the house so I can breathe again. Do you know, he even told me I was stacking the dishwasher wrong the other day? Since when has he ever shown any interest in household tasks and now he's an expert?"

She takes another slug of her wine and before I can comment we hear, "There you are."

We jump up as we see nan approaching, hand in hand with quite frankly a carbon copy of Finn, his best friend, Harvey Boston-granger.

Nan looks as if all her Christmas's have rolled into one as he kisses her hand and lowers her into a vacant chair and grins. "So, this is what you do with your time, is it? Lounge about and drink alcohol. No wonder you left the job, Finn, you are living the dream."

Finn jumps up and I watch as they hug it out and I can see the genuine happiness in their eyes as they greet one another.

Hanging back a little, I study Harvey and once again marvel at the force of nature that Finn calls his best friend. So good looking he should come with a government health warning. He has dark, close cropped hair and deep, dark eyes. His body could rival Hercules and he must be over 6 feet tall. Just standing in front of the sun makes it dark already and his biceps could occupy a room of their own. It's almost too much when they are in the same space because Finn on his own is mouth wateringly tasty but the two of them together is the stuff of dreams.

I watch with amusement as Heidi straightens up and fluffs out her hair and nan giggles like a teenage girl faced with her first crush. Mum looks a little brighter and Harvey beams around and then his gaze falls on me and I swallow – hard.

"Lily, my love, don't do it. I've come to save you from the beast who has captured you and hidden you away in the land that time forgot. I have a helicopter on standby, just say the word and we will run away together."

"Hi, Harvey."

I roll my eyes and he scoops me up, lifting me clean off the ground and whispers, "Looking good gorgeous. I meant every word."

"Back off man before I show you who's boss."

Laughing, Harvey lowers me to the ground and winks as Finn hands him a beer from the cooler.

"It's good to see you man. You're early, I wasn't expecting you until later."

"Yeah, I got a lift from a friend who has family in Nice."

He leans back and smiles good naturedly. "So, who do we have here then?"

His eyes zone in on Heidi who suddenly looks extremely hot and he winks. "Please tell me you're the bridesmaid because you know what they say..."

Heidi blushes furiously as Finn laughs. "Yeah, well you're out of luck because she's already taken and to answer your question, yes she is the bridesmaid."

Shrugging, he leans across and whispers something to Heidi, which makes her look as if she's about to implode on the spot and I watch as she grabs her wine and almost downs it in one.

Grandad says with interest, "You remind me of myself when I was a young man."

Nan spits her wine out and laughs. "Are you dreaming again, Bert, because take it from me, you were never remotely like him? Sad but true."

She grins and I can't help but laugh as mum says with interest, "So, Harvey, tell me, are you still single?"

"Mum!"

I feel mortified as she shrugs, "What's wrong with that, it's just a question?"

Laughing, he leans forward and stares into her eyes. "I'm saving myself."

"What for?"

Mum looks interested and Finn rolls his eyes as Harvey says, "For a woman as amazing as you but it's always my luck they are taken already."

Mum smiles and I note the sparkle in her eyes that definitely wasn't there a minute ago and shake my head, noting that dad looks a little put out.

Heidi catches my eye and raises hers and my heart sinks. Even she has *that* look which is bad news for Thomas because even I know nobody compares to these guys. They are a force of nature and hard to ignore. When I met Finn, I had the same reaction and who wouldn't? They are the kind of men who women dream of finding and when their attention turns to you, it's as if the whole world stops spinning and they are the only thing in it. Heidi has the same look in her eye that I had when I met Finley, so I say loudly, "When did you say Thomas was arriving, Heidi?"

I stare at her pointedly and feel a little surprised when she blushes and won't look in me in the eye, before saying dismissively, "I'm not sure exactly."

Before I can press her further, Harvey says loudly, "Well, until he does, I'll make it my mission to look after you."

Heidi looks as if she may just pass out on the spot and nan shakes her head. "Lucky cow."

Grandad rolls his eyes and reaches for another beer and I start to worry about his alcohol levels and say quickly, "Maybe we should rustle up something to eat to soak up this alcohol. Do you want to help me, Heidi?"

I stare at her pointedly and she looks as if it's the last thing she wants to do but nods. "Yes, of course."

Mum scrapes back her chair and I say quickly, "Don't worry mum, we've got this. You just relax a little, it's been a busy morning and I'll need your help later."

I nod imperceptibly towards Heidi and mum sits down and smiles. "Well, if you're sure."

Linking arms with my best friend, I pull her away from the group towards the castle because something isn't right with my best friend and I want answers and fast.

♥6

"It's nothing."

Heidi looks down and concentrates on making a salad and I sigh. "Listen, babe, I know you better than anyone and something is definitely up."

"Why do you think that?"

"Because normally you can't stop talking about Thomas and I don't think you've mentioned his name once since you've arrived."

Watching her carefully, I see her cheeks turn a little red and know she's hiding something as she shrugs, "It's nothing, really."

"Then tell me."

I stare at her with my best frown and she sighs and pushes the salad bowl away and I'm startled to see tears in her eyes.

"It didn't work out."

"What do mean, didn't work out? You've been together longer than Finn and I and only last week you were telling me how happy you were, what changed?"

She looks so sad my immediate response is to pull her in for a hug and I feel concerned as her shoulders shake as she says in a whisper, "It turned out he was cheating on me with his ex-girlfriend."

I hold her a little tighter and feel my heart twist in pain on her behalf. She sobs, "I found out by accident. He was in the shower and his phone rang, so I went to answer it but the answering machine kicked in and I heard her."

"What did she say?" Part of me hopes she's mistaken and what she tells me can be easily explained but she sighs and says in a small voice, "She told him their trip was arranged and to let me know the minute he had finished with me. She couldn't wait to see him and the last few weeks had been torture knowing he was with me."

The anger claws at my reasoning and I feel every bit as betrayed as she must feel. Then she says, "Thomas came out and heard her saying she loved him and the look on his face said it all. He was caught, tried and sentenced by that one phone call and obviously realised there was no hiding it, so he just said in a guilty voice that he was sorry and hadn't meant for it to happen but they had bumped into each other in Sainsburys two months ago and it was still there – the love they once had for each other and he had tried to put her out of his mind but couldn't."

She sits down and says sadly, "So that's it in a nutshell. Two wasted years of my life and one failing business because of it."

"What do you mean, I thought your mum was standing in for you when you went travelling?"

"Exactly. You know what she's like, Lily, she just can't help herself. She took over and thought she knew best. She made some terrible mistakes and her customer services skills are not the best there is and gradually the customers stopped coming."

"I'm so sorry, Heidi, I never knew."

"Why would you? I didn't know myself until two weeks ago. The business was an albatross I was keen to shift because Thomas and I were thinking about backpacking around Australia anyway but Thomas – well, that may take a bit longer to adjust to."

Sitting beside her, I take her hand in mine and say softly, "So, what are you going to do?"

"I'm not sure. I thought coming here would help remove me from the situation and make things clearer. It was the perfect distraction and I'm a great believer in things happening for a reason and fate deciding the road for you."

My eyes mist over as I think about my friend and the fact her happiness has evaporated along with the steam in Thomas's shower. Trying to be upbeat, I smile. "At least you know, that's the main thing and now you can start a fresh page in Heidi Monroe's journey through life. Maybe you should use and abuse Harvey while you're here. I'm sure he'd be up for it and you could do with something hot and heavy to take your mind off it."

Heidi smiles through her tears and nods. "He is rather gorgeous, isn't he?"

"Obviously."

"It wouldn't hurt anyone."

"No, of course not."

"Do you think he likes me?"

I shrug. "Harvey likes a pretty girl and you, my crazy friend, are one of the prettiest girls I know.

Yes, maybe a fling with Harvey is just what the doctor ordered. It will be fun to watch."

"You are not watching." Heidi's expression is full of alarm and I dissolve into a fit of the giggles. "Ew, as if. No, I meant watching him charm and sweep you off your feet. That will be fun to watch. Word of advice, though, don't make it easy on him. Men like Harvey love a challenge. They need to believe they don't have everything their own way and *that* will be the fun bit to watch."

Shaking her head, Heidi looks a little brighter as she carries on chopping the tomatoes. "Maybe you're right, Lily. He could be just the distraction I need and it may give me some self-respect back."

Turning away, I feel my heart sinking. What if he doesn't and isn't interested? She would be even more depressed than she is already. Once again, I think back to my mum's story and feel irritated. It's because of the curse, I just know it is. The fact that Heidi broke up with Thomas two weeks ago doesn't matter. I know that my mum's stupid story is responsible and I just hope it ends now because this is supposed to be the happiest time of my life and nothing is going to plan at all.

Later I get a chance to explain what happened to Finn and he looks as surprised as I was. "No way, I thought they would follow us down the aisle, poor Heidi."

"I know, but maybe it's for the best. At least she can dust herself off and find someone new before wasting the best years of her life on a cheater."

Finn places his arm around me and says thickly, "I will never be that guy, Lily. You are the only one I want and I will devote my whole life to making you happy."

Snuggling into him, I relish being by his side, but even I know life sometimes has other plans.

"At the moment you do, but what if we grow apart? You may decide I annoy you after a while and you actually realise that I'm not the amazing woman you think I am."

"I never said you were amazing."

He winks and I roll my eyes. "Keep pretending you don't idolise me, Finn, we both know you do."

He grins and then says with concern, "What about the dress, you never told me the full story."

"It's fine, I'm over it."

I turn away because I don't want him to see how devastated I am because that dress was *everything*. Of all the things that make up this wedding, that was the one I wanted the most. Now I'll be dressed up like Pollyanna and Finn may not think I'm so amazing then.

Sighing, I plaster on my brave face and say brightly, "Come on. Let's head downstairs and keep the guests fed and watered. Tonight is the easy one because when your family arrive, it could descend into the War of the Roses."

He groans, "Did we have to invite them?"

"Of course, they are still your parents."

"I know but maybe we didn't think this through. I always thought we should have run off and got married abroad, then we could have avoided a lot of trouble."

"Are you saying you're dreading this wedding?" I feel the pain hit me like a bat on a cricket ball and he says quickly, "Of course not, you know this my dream as much as yours. I'm just dreading my parents being in the same country with me in the middle."

"Is your dad…?"

Groaning again, he shakes his head. "I don't think so, hopefully he's coming alone."

I smile at him sympathetically because Finley's parents are in the middle of a very messy break up, largely due to the fact his father is having a mid-life crisis on top of another one and has decided he no longer wants Finn's mother and has discovered the joys of online dating. I've lost count of the number of dates he's had and all of them apparently with young girls in their twenties. It's all a little embarrassing really, and Finn's mum is bitter to say the least. I just hope he hasn't brought his latest as a plus one because if he has, it will ruin the whole thing.

Feeling bad for him, I smile brightly. "It will be fine; my mum will keep yours occupied and dad will help out with your father and your grandparents will be here and I'm sure they will keep things under control."

Finn shakes his head and says wearily, "Come on, I need some of that French wine we've been hoarding to dull the pain. Let's just have a relaxing night before they arrive when I'll be on edge the whole time."

As he takes my hand, I fight down the sinking feeling that's growing by the second. It all seemed like such a good idea at the time. A wedding in the south of France at the Castle of Dreams. Our home and the place we fell in love. It would have been perfect except for the emotional baggage that comes with inviting the family. Now I can only hope that they leave it back in England because I don't want anything else to go wrong.

♥ 7

The trouble with having several vineyards on your doorstep is the fact the wine is more in abundance than water and it appears that my guests are extremely dehydrated. After drowning our sorrows in several bottles of wine, I am very relieved when my nan and granddad decide to call it a night and stand to leave. Nan appears to be very shaky on her legs which isn't unusual when she's sober but now she's two sheets to the wind she'll need a mobility scooter to get her upstairs. Grandad appears to have lost his vision and keeps on telling her to stop jumping around all over the place and can't she stand in one spot long enough for him to grab her hand.

The rest of us laugh fit to burst as Harvey and Finn take charge and help them from the rather romantic looking garden. Harvey by sweeping my nan into his strong arms and carrying her away like a princess and Finn by supporting grandad as he tries to walk in a straight line.

Watching them go, Heidi giggles as nan's voice wafts towards us. "Ooh, Harvey, if I were ten years younger, you wouldn't leave my room tonight."

Mum looks at us in astonishment. "Did she really just say that? David, tell your mother not to make inappropriate comments to a guest at your daughter's wedding, she should know better."

"As if I could tell my mother anything, she's never listened in her life, let alone now."

"I see you inherited your own inability to listen from her then."

"Did you say something?"

We all crack up and mum nods. "See, never listens. You know, I think you need a hearing aid, David, most of what I say falls on deaf ears."

"Pardon?"

Dad holds his hand to his ear and we laugh as mum says slightly annoyed, "This is typical of you, David. Making light of a very serious situation."

She turns to Heidi and me and lowers her voice. "I keep on telling him to get those ears checked out. You know the amount of times I've asked him to do something and he says I never."

I see dad wink at us over her shoulder and fight back the laughter as mum looks annoyed. "They say it all starts to deteriorate when you retire and he is living proof of that. I mean, he's snored all his life but lately it's like going to bed in a storm and having the thunder snuggle down with you. He forgets what he's meant to be doing and if I send him out for something, he comes back with totally the wrong things. He doesn't remember anything I tell him and I'm not going to lie, I'm worried."

Rolling his eyes behind her back, dad grins and reaching out, pulls her towards him and in one superhuman move, lifts her off her feet and starts dancing around the patio to the sounds of Robbie Williams Angels.

Mum starts giggling and Heidi and I watch them in surprise as they glide effortlessly around and appear to shut the world out.

"How romantic."

Heidi sighs beside me and I see what she means. Mum is resting her head on dad's shoulder and as they sway in the moonlight underneath the stars, nothing could be more romantic. There is a gentle breeze calming the burn of the savage sun from earlier and the scent of jasmine hangs in the air. The music is low but loud enough to sing along to and the candles that burn for attention among the various fairy lights that light up the veranda, make it the most romantic of stages.

Heidi sighs beside me and I know she is thinking of Thomas and feel bad for her. Reaching out, I grab her hand and say softly, "Are you ok?"

She smiles bravely but even in the dim light I see the sadness in her eyes illuminated by the nearby candle flickering in the breeze and she shrugs, "I'll have to be. Life will go on, just not in the direction I thought it would. If anything, seeing your parents tonight reminds me that love is worth fighting for. I don't want to settle for second best when my soulmate is out there somewhere. I want what they have, Lily. I want a shared life with someone who loves me unconditionally without one eye on the horizon waiting for something better to come along. You have found that with Finn and if I'm honest, I knew deep down Thomas wasn't that man. I tried to pretend he was and that we were happy, but I knew."

"Knew what beautiful?"

We look up and see Harvey and Finn walking towards us and Heidi laughs with a little embarrassment. "I knew I shouldn't have drunk so much wine, I'll pay for it in the morning."

Reaching out, he pulls her to her feet in one swift move and as she falls against his chest, his arm pulls her tightly against him and he says huskily, "May I have the pleasure?"

Heidi's face is a picture as he proceeds to spin her around the patio, and Finn grins as he pulls me to my feet and does the same as his best friend. Feeling slightly anxious, I whisper, "She will be ok with him, won't she?"

Finn laughs softly and his breath tickles my ear as he whispers, "Relax, Harvey may not look like it but he's the perfect gentleman. Heidi will be fine, it's only a dance, after all."

He pulls me tightly against him and as I settle into his familiar hold, I relax for the first time since they all arrived. Finn has a habit of doing that. He takes your anxiety and crushes it to dust with his relaxed approach to life. He takes the edge off a tense situation and as I snuggle into him, I love the fact his arms hold me so safely keeping the world away. He kisses the top of my head and as I raise my lips to his, I love the way he kisses them softly and almost with a laziness that promises that time has no meaning for us. We have all the time in the world to enjoy what we have because he makes me feel secure and as if nothing bad could ever happen. Nothing bad ever does when I'm in his arms, which is why these moments are so special to me. It's the time when I'm at my happiest and as he spins me around the dancefloor, I am lost in the moment and shut the world out.

I don't even notice mum and dad steal away into the shadows without even saying goodnight. Maybe they did, but I am so wrapped up in Finn I don't even notice. I don't register that the song changes and the candles burn a little lower because I don't want to leave the comfort of these arms holding me securely in an increasing storm. And as I lose myself in Finn's kiss, I shut the world out and only when I open my eyes and the music ends, do I notice that we're alone and stare at him in shock and say fearfully, "Please don't tell me Heidi left with Harvey."

Looking around, it's evident we are the only ones here and Finn shrugs. "I saw them leave but don't worry, I told you, he's the perfect gentleman, she's safe with him."

Worrying that it may be the other way around, I say fearfully, "What if she's so upset over Thomas, she lets her guard down and does something she regrets in the morning? It will be so awkward during the wedding if the bridesmaid and best man have issues."

"Issues, what are you talking about?"

"You know what I'm talking about. What if they… you know, and she regrets it? You see, Heidi isn't that sort of girl, Finn. She's got a strong moral compass that only goes off course when the alcohol distorts her purpose."

"What are you talking about?" Finn starts to laugh and I say tightly, "It's all very well for you to laugh but women are very different to men. I'm sure Harvey would only be too happy to take advantage of a pretty woman in turmoil, but Heidi wouldn't be able to live with the shame."

"You've had too much to drink again, nothing like that will happen, and if it did, I'm guessing Heidi wouldn't be upset about it either."

Thinking about Harvey Boston-granger, I'm pretty sure she wouldn't, after all, he's not even human and Finn whispers, "Think back to that crazy bucket list mission you were on when we met. It had some pretty amazing things on it that I'm sure you wouldn't have dreamed of doing but now look back on as the best moments of your life. If I remember, kissing a stranger under the stars, was one of them and sleeping with a stranger on a beach the other."

"That was different."

"How was it? Surely if you learned anything from that experience it was that life's too short to overthink things. The magic in life comes from those unexpected moments that bring the life to your soul. If you hadn't been so intent on completing that list of your Aunts, we wouldn't be here now. Do you regret any of it? I doubt it because all of those little memories are tied up inside your mind and filed in a special place. They are the memories you will reach for later in life that will mean so much. Not the general day to day living we enjoy, but those unexpected moments that bring the greatest pleasure. Don't be worried if your friend experiences a few of them for herself because right now she needs a little bit of crazy to get her through."

"Yes, but…"

Finn silences my words with a firm finger on my lips and looks deeply into my eyes. "I love you Lily Rose Adams and the woman I fell in love with didn't let life hold her back. She was fearless and independent and knew her own mind. Let Heidi find that person inside her when she needs it the most and just be happy that someone like Harvey is on hand to protect her integrity."

As he says the words, we both start to laugh because the thought of Harvey Boston-granger being the guardian of integrity is more of a fairy tale than the one we are living right now. The candles flicker and the silence fills the air as the music stops, Finn reaches for my hand and says huskily, "Come on, let's worry about it tomorrow. Tonight belongs to us."

As we blow out the remaining candles and head upstairs to our romantic turret in the Castle of Dreams, I am reminded once again of how lucky I was to find this man who walks beside me. Nothing can ever go wrong when Finn's around. If I know anything, it's that.

♥ *8*

Heidi won't look me in the eye, Harvey looks extremely pleased with himself, mum and dad are still nursing hangovers and nan and grandad have decided to have breakfast in bed.

Catching Finn's eye, I shake my head and he grins before heading off with Harvey for a workout.

Seizing the opportunity, I grab my best friend and say in a 'she means business' voice, "Well?"

"Well, what?"

"What happened last night, of course? You sloped off with Harvey before I knew you'd gone and now you have that look on your face."

"What look?"

"You know full well what I mean and now you're stalling. Come on, did you, or did you not, sleep with Harvey last night?"

"Maybe, maybe not," She shrugs and I stare at her with frustration.

"Oh no missy, cryptic answers not allowed. It's my house, ok castle, my wedding and my rules."

"What are you, my mother?"

"No, just a very concerned bride who is fearful that her maid of honour has already sampled the best man before the speeches are even written."

Sighing, Heidi pushes away her plate and fixes me with a smug look and my heart sinks. "You didn't."

My voice reflects my despair and she laughs. "Of course not, although I wouldn't say no if he asked."

"What you mean?"

I stare at her incredulously as she rolls her eyes.

"I'm not saying I wasn't tempted, after all, that man was sent by the devil to ruin pure souls everywhere but he was the perfect gentleman, more's the pity. After we left, we walked a little around the lake and held hands and it was kind of romantic. I even considered kissing him to see what it would feel like, but somehow it didn't feel right. I mean, obviously I'm still getting over one love of my life and it would be bad to jump straight into a fling with someone else, so we just talked and laughed and drank in the atmosphere and enjoyed the serenity living here brings."

"But what happened next? I mean, you won't look me in the eye."

"The thing is, Lily, I knew what you were thinking and I would be the same. Part of me would love to tell you I spent a wild night of passion with Harvey but I didn't and it's the part of me that's disappointed about that I'm struggling to come to terms with."

"What do you mean?"

Heidi looks so sad it tears at my heartstrings and she says sadly. "The fact I even wanted to upsets me more than anything. It showed me that what I had with Thomas over the past two years was obviously meaningless. If I truly loved him, I wouldn't even want to talk to another man, let alone crave intimacy with one I've just met. I suppose I didn't want to look at you because of all the people that know me, you can see inside my soul and I'm not sure I like the person that's living there at the moment."

She looks down and I feel bad for her but on the one hand I'm happy because it shows that she will be ok. She will move on and up and if not with Harvey then someone else.

Nudging her, I say with amusement, "I bet he tried though."

"Actually no, do you think that's because he doesn't fancy me?"

She looks a little hurt and I shake my head vigorously. "Of course, he fancies you, who wouldn't? He's just behaving himself and being a gentleman. You know, they may look as if they break women's hearts for fun, but these guys have a strong moral code they live by. Harvey may play the joker and flirt terribly, but he is a decent guy underneath it all."

Heidi smiles and I can see in her eyes she has some feelings for Harvey because just the mention of his name meant she hung onto every word I said. Maybe they will get together. Stranger things have happened and we do live in the Castle of Dreams, after all. Perhaps Heidi was always meant to find her future here and the same for Harvey. I certainly hope so because it would all work out perfectly if it did, my best friend with Finn's. Immediately I see the pluses with none of the minuses and picture cosy evenings double dating and watching films. They would marry and then we would have our children at the same time and raise them to be best friends too. Maybe they would come and live with us and we could convert one of the gites. Yes, the more I think about it the more I like the idea, so I smile brightly and say happily. "Well, it will be interesting to see what happens. Now, I'm sorry to leave you but I must get ready to receive my second wave of visitors and they will not be as easy as the first."

"Why, who's coming?"

"Finley's family and quite honestly Heidi, things are about to go downhill and fast."

"Why, they can't be that bad, surely? I mean, Finn is a treasure."

"You'll see."

I turn away and she says quickly, "Let me help. Just tell me what to do and I'll be your assistant."

"Ok, you can help make sure their rooms are ready and then we can make a start on lunch. I'm sure if we feed them with enough food and wine, they will need to sleep it off and leave us to enjoy some peace and quiet."

As we set about making their rooms comfortable, I think about Finn's mum. Stella Roberts is one of those women who make the rest of us feel inadequate. She is always well groomed and immaculate and never speaks out of turn or says anything bad about anyone. She has a no-nonsense approach and always tries to help out where she can. As far as I can see, her only fault is she thinks she's always right and it makes me smile as I think of her because I know another woman very much like her who married Stella's nephew Arthur. A very good friend of mine Sable who I owe a lot to and along with her husband, owns half of the Chateau of Dreams with Finn and I. Yes, I can see why Arthur fell in love with Sable because she is a mirror image of all the women in his family.

I feel a deep longing to see my friend because Sable approaches life with a can-do attitude. She is arriving tomorrow with Arthur and then I can breathe a little easier because she is taking over as soon as she gets here. I have left my wedding in capable hands and she will know what to do. I imagine she would have sniffed out my dress in that shop and not left until we had it. Yes, Sable is the type of woman the rest of us aspire to be and tomorrow can't come soon enough for me.

It's what happens today that's worrying me.

9

"We're here." Mum looks up sharply and catches my eye and my heart sinks.

Pasting a smile on my face, I stand and head towards the guests who have made their way outside, led by a beaming Finn who was sent to collect them from the airport.

"Stella, you look amazing as always."

I gloss over the fact she looks tired and a little pale as I kiss her three times, as has become the protocol with her.

She stands back and rakes a critical eye over me and says firmly, "Lily, you look in need of help. Those eyes tell me you need some sleep and there's a hint of weariness in your expression that tells me it's all too much for you."

I can see my mum bristling behind her and smile. "Oh, we just had a late night and drank too much wine. To be honest, we're all feeling it a bit today."

Stella raises a well-plucked eyebrow and then turns her attention to my mum. "Sonia, darling, how lovely you look."

I watch them air kiss and note a slight decrease in tension as Stella says warmly, "You, on the other hand, look positively radiant. Whatever you were drinking last night certainly agrees with you, which means it will be my drink of choice tonight."

Mum looks pleased at the compliment and then dad steps forward and kisses Stella on the cheek.

"It's good to see you, Stella. Can I get you a glass of something to take the edge off your journey?"

He leads Stella away and mum says softly, "Do you think she's had Botox?"

"What makes you say that?"

"Her expression. There was no emotion there. She smiled but nothing moved. Classic giveaway if you ask me."

I stare after Stella in surprise, "Maybe, I'll ask Finn if he knows."

Mum snorts. "As if. No, darling, men don't know these things because women don't like to admit to the vanity women of our age feel when we're faced with withering looks. Why do you think the cosmetics companies make such huge profits because we will pay anything to make the outside mirror the inside?"

"Mum, what are you talking about, you look amazing?"

"I know, but it's not down to nature. No, I have a very strict skin care regime that has developed over the years. I drink lots of water and make sure I work out because if I didn't I would be on the slippery slope. If you ask me, Stella is doing a spot of high maintenance herself, although it's a little like shutting the stable door after the horse has bolted."

"Mum!" I stare at her in disbelief as she shrugs.

"Well, I heard Piers has already traded her in for a newer model, several times over. Poor woman is probably so depressed she's trying to compete and win back his affections. You know, it wouldn't surprise me if foul play is involved further down the line when things come to a head."

"Stop it mum, there will be no foul play and just because Finn's parents have decided to go their separate ways, it doesn't mean Stella is trying to win him back by making herself look younger. She may have her eye on a younger model herself. Maybe she's the one with a string of admirers and Piers will regret his haste in moving on. What about that? Shall we go and ask what nan thinks?"

Mum looks thoughtful. "Maybe we should check on them. Do you think they died in their sleep after drinking too much, I wouldn't be surprised?"

"Don't even say such a thing, you know, sometimes mum your mouth forms words before your brain agrees to release them. Don't say anything about death for the rest of the time you're here."

I stomp off and as I pass, Finn pulls me across to say hi to his father and I smile as he pulls me in for a hug. "My gorgeous soon to be daughter-in-law. I'm so happy that my son found a good one to spend his life with."

Pulling back, I smile brightly. "Hi, Piers, you're looking good as always."

He winks and it strikes me just how good looking he is. It's no wonder Finn is so gorgeous with parents like his. Piers nods. "Thanks, I like to keep with the times. You know, the past few months have really opened my eyes to how things have changed. To be honest, I used to dread change, but I must say I'm loving it now. The digital age is the best one yet and I'm enjoying exploring everything it has to offer."

Heidi walks past and my heart sinks as Piers whispers, "Who is that gorgeous creature?"

Finn sighs as I say firmly, "My best friend Heidi and leave her alone because she's in a vulnerable state right now and needs to be left to heal."

Piers looks after her with a thoughtful expression and my heart sinks. Finn looks apologetic as he says loudly, "Come on dad, I'll take you to meet the others and then fix you a drink. When did you say nan and grandad were arriving?"

"Not long after us, I think. Mind you, they have never been reliable and could turn up when it's all over."

Finn shakes his head. "I told them I'd be happy to go and meet them but you know what they're like, they won't accept help from anyone."

We all share a smile because Finn's grandparents, Oscar and Betty are the sort of people you never get tired of. Good company, fun to be around and not a bad bone in their bodies. They currently live in Spain where they retired years ago and are flying in later tonight to make up Finn's side of the family. The last guests we're waiting for are Sable and Arthur and my brother Mark. They all arrive tomorrow but until then I need to settle the new arrivals in, so say over my shoulder, "Stella, would you like me to show you to your room?"

She nods and breaks off from talking to mum and heads towards us as Finn whispers, "I'll sort dad out."

As we walk away, Stella sighs heavily and lowers her voice.

"You know, Lily, I am dreading being around Piers so much."

My heart sinks. "I'm sure it will be fine."

My voice sounds bright but I don't feel it inside and Stella shakes her head. "It's been a difficult time and as you know, things have been a little strained between us. Luckily, he stays at the flat in London most of the time, leaving me to come to terms with things in Guildford. But people talk, darling and they love nothing more than telling me all about his latest toys and rubbing my nose in the fact he is getting on with life without me and it hurts."

Taking her arm, I try to offer her the only comfort I know how because it must be the hardest thing to live through and she shakes her head. "Do you know, a small part of me was hoping that this wedding would make him look at things differently."

My heart breaks as I hear the hope in her voice and realise she still loves him. "Is that what you want?"

"Yes, I think I do. Don't get me wrong, darling, I'm so angry with him most of the time but I can't shake that part of me that would forgive him in a heartbeat if he told me he wanted to come back to me. Why can't I break free of my feelings for him? He's publicly humiliated me, is indiscreet with his women and appears to be having the time of his life. He thinks that because I have the house and most of our disposal income, I am happy, but how can I be when he isn't by my side? Do you think I'm weak, Lily?"

My eyes fill with tears for her and I say sadly, "You can't help how you feel, Stella. Who knows what the future will bring, but until then you must do what's best for you before anything else? Maybe this will be an ordeal for you but maybe it will help you come to terms with how things are now and who knows, it may all change back again."

"Do you think so?"

I hear the hope in her voice and feel annoyed because I had no right to give her any "I'm not sure but whatever happens, you will be ok. If it's not Piers, there is someone out there for you and we just need to find him."

We reach the room I prepared for her and she looks around in delight.

"Lily, I love it!"

As she wanders around, I see her taking in every detail and I feel a surge of pride as I see the room through her eyes. White silk curtains billow in the breeze as the open window looks down over the rose garden below. White-washed walls provide a simple canvas for the beautiful art that decorates them and a brass bed stands proudly on a soft pale blue carpet, filled with decorative cushions dressing the simple white bedding that was a steal on Brand alley. Mirrored furniture sparkles in the sunlight and the door that leads through to the ensuite, shows a clean, modern bathroom that is dressed with all the comforts any guest would be happy to indulge in. Large white fluffy towels warm on the chrome heated towel rail. Baskets of luxurious cosmetics promise indulgence and a white towelling robe and slippers wait patiently nearby for the occupant to shrug off their clothes and soak in a steamy, scented bath, while sampling the complimentary wine that stands next to the scented candle on the side along with two glasses.

Feeling a little worried that I forgot and put two glasses out, I wonder if I can hide one of them before Stella notices but she sees them almost immediately and I see a shadow cross her face as she sighs and then shakes herself before saying happily, "I love what you've done with the place. Congratulations darling, this place will attract so many people you will be busy for years."

I feel a warm feeling spreading through me at her praise and look around with pride. Yes, we have worked hard and this was the fun part. Drawing on my experience from working at Designer Homes - *on budget* for so many years, I pulled out all the stops to make the castle modern, yet romantic at the same time, on a very tight budget.

Stella kicks off her shoes and buries her feet in the luxurious carpet and sighs. "You know, Lily, if I go missing at all this is where I'll be. In fact, I may not even leave the room, this is amazing."

Smiling, I look around before saying brightly, "Then I'll leave you to settle in. I really should check on my grandparents, they've slept in far too long already and I need them to join us for lunch which will be ready in half an hour."

Stella nods and I leave her to unpack and head across the hallway to the room I allocated my grandparents. The stairs aren't a problem for them yet and I did think about putting them in the little gîte next door but nan said she wanted to stay in the castle itself. Instead, I've put Finn's grandparents in the gîte next to Harvey, who occupies the neighbouring one. Finn is going to share with him the night before the wedding to keep at least one tradition alive and it seemed the best idea because then technically he isn't under the same roof as me.

Once again, a delicious feeling spreads through me as I think of marrying Finn in just a few days' time. It actually can't come soon enough for me because it's all I want – him.

10

"Are you awake?"

I knock loudly on my grandparent's door and press my ear to it to hear if there are any signs of life. I feel a little anxious because they have been asleep for rather a long time. Despite the fact they are fit and healthy, they are in their seventies and it worries me.

Hearing nothing, I try the handle and feel nervous as it turns because it feels wrong to intrude on their privacy.

However, as I open the door a fraction, I see the light streaming through the crack and know they must be up at least because the curtains are drawn, so I say a little louder, "Nan, grandad, are you here?"

There is still no reply, so I edge inside and look around in surprise.

They're not here.

The bed is made and as usual the room is neat and tidy.

Wandering around, I check the bathroom. "Nan, granddad, are you here?"

There is nothing but the gentle sounds of nature outside their window and I wonder if I missed them and they are downstairs already.

As I turn to leave, mum pokes her head around the door. "Are they here?"

"No, apparently not, did you see them downstairs?"

"If I did, I wouldn't be asking."

She looks irritable and I'm starting to realise that she hasn't been herself since she arrived and taking my chance say softly, "Is everything ok, mum?"

"What do you mean?"

She sighs impatiently and I say gently, "It's just that you don't seem yourself. Is there anything bothering you?"

Mum sighs and heads into the room, clicking the door shut behind her and sinks down on the chair near the window. I perch on the end of the bed opposite and wait for her to speak, a knot of worry forming inside as I see the pain in her eyes.

"I'm sorry, Lily, darling, but I'm struggling a little. You see, when your father retired, I thought our new life would all be champagne and roses. But it's not. He has settled into becoming some sort of layabout while I still continue to fetch and carry for him as I've always done. He gets up late and expects breakfast to be served to him, while he wastes another hour trawling through the papers. Then he follows me around the house while I try to clean and moans that he's bored and can we go to the garden centre for a coffee? Then he expects lunch, which quite frankly isn't that soon after I've cleared away the breakfast things. Occasionally he'll potter in the garden but then keeps on calling for refreshing drinks because he's 'working' and expects me to drop everything. He has this annoying habit of standing at the back door and shouting for me and keeps on calling even if I've answered him a hundred times already. By the time the evening comes, he sits in front of the television and doesn't move all night, just flicking between the programmes and playing on his iPad simultaneously. I, meanwhile, am still clearing up and trying to do things like the ironing and planning for the next day while he complains that he's bored. This is on repeat every day and I am being driven slowly mad. You've got to help me, darling, he needs a job and fast because my love of midsommer murders is tainting my vision of our future. What if I'm driven to the same lengths and murder him in a fit of rage one day when he leaves the bloody toilet seat up yet again, or trip over his golf bag that he leaves lying in the hallway? I'm on the emotional edge, Lily and can't see a way out of it. Now I can see why people our age divorce at this time of their lives because when they are forced to spend actual time together, they realise the person they married never really grew up."

She stops for breath and I feel the weight of my parent's crumbling marriage sitting heavily on my shoulders. I'm not sure what to say because I'm shocked hearing her speak about my father like this. I always thought they were happy and the benchmark for couples everywhere. Is this what I can look forward to? A lifetime of caring for my husband only to resent it later on in life.

Feeling worried, I try to brush it under the new carpet and say brightly, "Maybe this is the break you both need. You know, a break from the normal routine somewhere different. If I were you, I would encourage him in the golfing thing and if not, find some other hobby to occupy his time. Maybe you can find a joint one that will bring you closer together, you know, a shared love of something like gardening, walking or visits to the National Trust."

Mum groans and shakes her head. "No, darling, he needs something that will get him from under my feet giving me my personal space back. I'm struggling to remember why I married him in the first place and don't know what to do about it."

Feeling extremely worried and hating the part of me that's annoyed at her for bringing her emotional baggage to my wedding, I say brightly, "Let's go and find nan and grandad. If anyone knows the secret to a happy marriage, it's them."

Nodding, mum stands and then says apologetically. "I'm sorry, darling, I didn't mean to cast a shadow over your big day. Maybe we should just forget I said it. Concentrate on your happiness instead because I *am* happy for you, you know that. Finn is a remarkable man and I can tell he makes you happy. Don't let my whining spoil what is set to be a magical wedding and just let me work something out like I always have done."

Suddenly, she smiles and I notice a light enter her eyes as she says excitedly, "Anyway, Mark is due in the morning and I can't wait. It's been so long, maybe it's just the tonic I need. Come on, darling, let's go and forget I said anything and crack open the wine and toast your future over a nice spread of charcuterie and French bread."

Marvelling at how my mum's moods can switch so readily, I follow her back to my guests and an increasingly complicated next few days.

Once the table is set and ready, I stand back and look on a French paradise. We set up the table in the orchard because it offers a little shade from the midday sun and provides a calming environment for a leisurely lunch of cold meats and salad with baskets of French bread set along the middle. Wine of every colour sits in carafes next to water bottles to quench our thirst as we indulge in some outdoors living. The white tablecloth flutters in the breeze and the polished cutlery sparkles beside the mismatched plates that were the result of scouring every French brocante fair in the district. Colourful cushions provide comfort on the metal chairs and as settings go, this one is as romantic as they come. We have set the chairs the length of one long table and everyone but nan and grandad are already seated, their gentle laughter wafting through the trees as they relax and enjoy the olives and crisps that provide an appetiser to the main event.

I feel a little worried as I see Harvey beside Heidi with his arm casually running along the back of her chair and note the sparkle in her eyes as she laughs at something he says. Stella is chatting to mum and at the opposite end of the table, dad and Piers are deep in conversation.

Suddenly, we hear, "Don't start without us."

Looking in the direction the voice came from, my heart lifts as I see my nan and grandad heading our way looking extremely pleased with themselves. Nan is wearing a bright yellow sundress and grandad looks resplendent in beige trousers with a polo shirt.

Mum says loudly, "Where have you been, we were worried?"

Beaming around at everyone, nan says lightly, "We were up early and fancied exploring. We went for a stroll and then hopped on a passing bus that took us to the town. You know, I've had such fun exploring the local shops and then we had a coffee in one of those little bistros."

Mum shakes her head as nan spies the new arrivals and says politely, "Hi, Stella, Piers, when did you get here?"

Stella smiles and nan sits beside her and I watch as they share an air kiss or three. "Not long ago, you're looking amazing, Sandra."

Nan looks pleased as grandad joins the men at the other end of the table and I leave them to it, taking my seat opposite Heidi as Finn sits beside me.

Lunch is a relaxed affair and I soon stop worrying about my mum's problems and just enjoy the banter being around Harvey and Finn brings. We talk about the wedding and everything that's been arranged and then Heidi says, "Are you going to have a hen night, Lily?"

"I doubt it, I mean, we haven't invited many people and it's so close now I wouldn't have the time."

Harvey shakes his head. "There's always time for the last night of freedom. When did you say the rest of the guests were arriving?"

"Tomorrow, everyone should be here by then."

I feel a little anxious as Harvey grins and I don't miss the wicked look he shares with Finn. "Great, then the day after tomorrow, make sure you have a lie in because that evening we will all enjoy a parting of the ways and the girls can go one way and the boys another."

"What are you thinking?"

Finn leans forward with interest and Harvey says thoughtfully, "Oh, just a few drinks in the local town. We could order a minibus and then go our separate ways when we're there. Nothing outrageous, just a few drinks. What do you say, Lily, do you fancy a night out with the girls?"

Heidi looks excited. "Oh, please say you will, Lily. We could have so much fun and I would love to be in charge of it. Leave it with me, I'll make it a night you will never forget."

Finn laughs and takes my hand and says fiercely. "You look after my girl, Heidi, don't lead her astray."

I catch the expression on Harvey's face and roll my eyes. "I think it's more like Harvey will lead you astray. Mind you, it would be nice to have a change of scene, so thanks, I'll leave the arrangements in your capable hands."

As they start to whisper to each other, Finn leans closer, "Are you ok with that?"

"I think so, after all, it's not as if anything could possibly go wrong in provincial France. It's hardly the metropolis."

He kisses me softly and my world rights itself. My last night of freedom means nothing to me. It's the day after that counts because I have been waiting for that day my whole life.

11

Life at a castle is never dull and there is always something to do. After a leisurely lunch we all help clear away the dishes and then the parents and grandparents decide on a gentle game of croquet on our perfect lawn. Harvey decides to head off for a run with Finn and Heidi and I take a gentle stroll around the lake and I am pleased to see that my friend is regaining some of her sparkle.

Linking arms, we walk slowly enjoying the sound of birdsong and the gentle lap of the waves and Heidi looks around and sighs, "I love it here, Lily, it's so far from Tooting we could be on another planet."

"Do you know what you'll do – with the business, I mean?"

I ask the question she is probably dreading because I know she was so excited when she opened her knitting shop and then she met Thomas and he became the most important thing in her life. Now both are all but gone and I wonder what she will do next.

"I don't know, really. I suppose after your wedding I'll return home and tie up any loose ends with the shop. After that, I'm not so sure."

Feeling sorry for my friend, I suddenly have an idea. "You know, Heidi, I can't believe I never thought of this before but why don't you come and work here for the summer? We are booked out nicely with guests and I could certainly use the help. You could live in one of the gites and take some time to think about your next step."

Heidi looks at me in astonishment and then her eyes fill with tears. You would do that – for me?"

"Why not? We need to hire some staff and I can think of nothing I would like more. Say you'll think about it at least."

She nods, her eyes shining brightly and then says happily, "I've thought about it and yes, the answer is yes, of course I'll be your servant."

Laughing, I roll my eyes. "Chance would be a fine thing. Knowing you, you'll soon step up and take charge and be ordering me around."

Suddenly, the air we breathe is a very different sort. It's fresher and more invigorating than before, with the promise of brighter times ahead. I can't believe I never thought of it before because with Heidi and Finn by my side, I can't fail.

For the rest of the walk, it's all we can talk about. We plan the rest of our year and laugh and chat like old times. Walking with Heidi is a tonic I didn't really know I needed until it happened. I've been so busy and wrapped up with the renovation and then the wedding, I almost haven't had time to breathe and I suppose it was all weighing heavily on my mind. Now it's as if I've let the light in and it feels good to have somebody I care for shouldering some of the burden ahead.

After a while, Heidi says with interest. "So, what's left to organise for the wedding? It's only a few days away and from what I can see you have it all under control."

"Not really."

"Why?"

"I haven't got a clue what's happening. I mean, you know me, I'm a great one for lists and planning. I have a whole box file for every room in the castle, as well as a corresponding notebook. When it came to my own wedding, I gave it all up to my wedding planner so I could concentrate on getting the castle ready."

"Why do I only know about this now? Who on earth is your wedding planner?"

"Sable, of course."

"Sable, but she's in London, how can she plan your wedding in France?"

"Honestly, Heidi, I thought you knew that woman can organise a wedding in Australia if she wanted to. No, we've had several Facetime calls and our own WhatsApp group purely for this occasion. She sends me over any ideas for approval and runs things past Finn and me before booking them. You know, she has been a godsend because she has left nothing to chance. When she arrives tomorrow, the wedding will come with her because if I know Sable Evans this will be a wedding to remember. All Finn and I had to do was make sure the castle is ready and our guests settled and Sable and Arthur – well, mainly Sable, will see to everything else."

Heidi looks impressed. "That's amazing, lucky you. Do you trust her enough with your wedding though, I mean, I know how much of a control freak you are?"

"Of course." I shrug and smile with a bravery that is diminishing with every step nearer the wedding we take. "Sable won't let me down; she knows how important this is to me and Finn."

We head back towards the castle and I try to push down any doubts I had about relinquishing control of the most important day of my life. The trouble is, since mum told me her stupid story, everything has been a little off. Finding out that my mum and dad are having problems was yet another blow and I wonder how many more I can cope with.

Later on, Finn's grandparents Oscar and Betty arrive by taxi and we are all waiting like a welcoming committee to greet them. Almost as soon as she steps foot from the taxi, Betty is running towards us, shouting, "There they are, my favourite couple in the world, let me look at you."

Finn laughs as she launches herself at him and then pulls me in for a hug as we hear, "Bloody hell, Betty, leave me to do all the work will you?"

We grin as Oscar stands by the car laughing as Harvey and Piers race forward to help him with their cases and Stella says in horror, "How long are you staying for, mum?"

It appears to be some time because one by one the largest suitcases appear and I wonder how they managed to fit them inside the taxi because they must have at least three each. Piers groans at the weight of one as Harvey lifts two larger ones with ease and Betty says in wonder, "Hey darling, you can come home with me."

Harvey winks and Betty giggles as Finn rolls his eyes. "Seriously though, nan, what's with all the luggage, didn't they have baggage limitations on that aircraft you flew in from Spain on?"

"There are no limitations where your grandmother is concerned, Finn. It cost me a bloody fortune in upgrading our seats and then paying excess."

Oscar grumbles but his eyes twinkle as he looks at Betty fondly and suddenly all hope is restored. This is what I want – what they have and now I see it's possible I feel a lot better.

As we walk inside the castle, Betty chatters non-stop and gasps with delight as she appreciates just about every attention to detail we have created. "Finn, I love this place, it's like a dream come true. You have done a magnificent job. I always knew you were a clever boy, but this – it's amazing."

Laughing, Finn squeezes my hand. "It's mainly down to Lily and her passion for interior design. I wouldn't know the first thing about choosing any of this stuff."

Betty looks at him fondly. "I'm sure you have other skills."

Turning to me, she winks and I stifle a giggle as Finn grins.

Having Finn's grandparents here is like a breath of fresh air wafting through the castle. Any anxieties or problems seem a lifetime away because positivity and fun follow them wherever they go.

Finn's other grandparents died a few years back and his mother's parents are the only ones he has left and I know he idolises them both. Now they're here, I can relax a little and just enjoy their company because we don't get to very often.

Finn helps Oscar with the cases and I show Betty the little gîte that Finn and I first stayed in when we met here all those years ago. I still have so many fond memories of the place and can't bear to change a thing about it. I did install some heating though and spruced up the interior a little but aside from that it is just how I remember it and of all the rooms here, this is still my favourite one.

As I settle them in, Betty looks around and smiles happily. "You know dear, this place has a simplicity to it that gives it far more value than a room dripping in gold."

I definitely agree with that and nod. "I just can't bear to change anything because this is where Finn and I fell in love."

"Ah, love, if you find the right man that feeling will never leave you. If anything, it starts as a seed and grows into something beautiful. Make sure you tend it well though, Lily, because if neglected it fades fast and soon dies."

"Wise words, Betty."

"Yes, I thought so too when I read them in the Mills & Boon I borrowed from the library and read on the plane over."

"She's always reading utter trash if you ask me."

Oscar groans as he sets the last case down and moves across to his wife and kisses her on the cheek to take the sting from his words.

"You don't complain, at least it keeps our passion alive." They share a look which is a little uncomfortable to watch and Finn visibly pales. Then I start to giggle as they begin ballroom dancing around the small kitchen, yelling, "Come on guys, join in, it's more fun that way."

Laughing, Finn crosses the room and I need no further invitation to take the hand he offers and allow his arms to fold around me. As we sway in time to his nan and grandad singing some song from the past, life feels so good. Finn kisses the top of my head and I congratulate myself on a good choice and a bright future.

♥ *12*

The alarm goes off at 6 am and Finn groans as I jump to attention.

"Oh my god, Finn, we must get up and ready they will be here soon."

"It's 6 am we've got hours."

"You may think that but by the time we've tidied up and prepared the castle for their arrival, they will be knocking on the door."

"It's not that bad, the others will help; relax and come back to bed."

Throwing a cushion at him, I struggle into my dressing gown. "In case you've forgotten, most of our guests will be a little worse for wear this morning. I think they drank us dry and I just hope we manage to re-stock in time for the wedding."

Finn laughs and I think back to the huge party that broke out last night. Oscar and Betty started off the singing and then gave dance lessons. Nan and grandad joined in and even mum and dad. Harvey was out-of-control dancing with all the ladies and Stella managed to avoid Piers for most of the evening until they were forced to dance together by Betty who wouldn't take no for an answer. The worst thing was watching Piers try to hit on Heidi, and I was grateful that Harvey stepped in and whisked her away in what appeared to be the Tango. I have a headache just thinking about the empty bottles downstairs and the food that was left until the morning because enjoying ourselves took precedent over domestic chores.

"Your mum and dad seemed to enjoy themselves."

"Yes, they've always enjoyed a slow dance."

My cheeks flame as I hop on one foot while I struggle into my slipper boots and dash for the bathroom because I have never been so embarrassed in my life.

Mum and dad took it upon themselves to demonstrate extreme Samba. Apparently, it's all the rage in Surbiton village hall and I didn't know where to look. All that thrusting and grinding was seriously interfering with my mental health and I'm not sure if I will ever shake the image of them making out on the dance floor.

Nan and grandad were trying to copy them until my nan's knees gave out and she had to be helped to her feet by Piers who then proceeded to swing her around the room causing me to wonder if they would make it to our wedding alive.

It must have been 2 am before they hobbled off to bed and I just hope they wake up and think about what they've done. Shocking behaviour if you ask me and I will be having stern words with them all when they resurface.

Once I've completed my morning facial routine of cleanse, tone, moisturise and meditate, five minutes later I'm ready for action. Pulling on my leggings and sweatshirt. I tie my hair in a ponytail and put my sliders on and head downstairs.

Finn just grunted and turned over and I just hope the alarm I set wakes him before I'm reduced to using the cold flannel treatment.

As I pass Heidi's door, I decide to knock and ask for her help because of everyone she seemed the most sober.

However, there's no answer which means she must still be asleep, so thinking nothing of it, I turn the handle and head inside. This is not unusual; we've always had an open-door policy, but I'm surprised to see her room is empty and the bed made already.

Feeling a little happier that I won't have to wake her myself, I head downstairs to fire up the kettle and make the first of many black coffees.

However, when I head into the kitchen, it's apparent I'm the first one, so I flick the switch on the kettle and look around me with despair.

This will take all day.

Dishes, empty glasses and discarded packaging litter my Italian granite surfaces. The bins are overflowing and I can't even see the sink for the number of pans in it. The dishwasher is full with dirty dishes and I feel a panic attack coming on.

This is a disaster because Sable will be here in about six hours and I will be hard pushed to make it look as if I'm managing by then. I envisioned myself greeting her with my guests all lined up on the edge of the garden, with a refreshing cocktail and canapes to welcome her. Her helicopter will land at precisely midday, which doesn't give me much time to arrange it. I even picked out my best summer dress for the occasion and imagined gliding around the castle showing her how well we were managing and proving that I am cut from the same cloth as she is. A powerful woman who knows the secret of getting things done. If she could see me now scrubbing pans and hauling the bins outside to the courtyard, she would be horrified.

As I work, I mutter curses under my breath and can't believe that I thought it was a good idea having everyone stay here. Is this really what it's like having paying guests? Will my life be an endless round of catering, washing, cooking and tidying up after people who should know better?

It must be an hour later that Finn surfaces and heads bleary eyed into the kitchen wearing sweat pants and nothing else. My mouth waters at the slightly messy hair that needs combing into place, preferably with my fingers and his muscles that ripple as he moves that have been perfected just for my own personal pleasure. Yes, Finn is a huge distraction for me because he is the sort of man women lust over and I am no exception, so it's no surprise that my anger vanishes the minute he pulls me into those strong arms and lowers his lips to mine and kisses me with a hunger that makes me think that everything else can wait. "Come back to bed."

His voice is husky and he presses his lips to mine and almost steals the breath from my body. Ordinarily I can refuse him nothing when he asks but the sight of the dishes over his shoulder for once take precedent and I groan, "I can't."

He kisses my neck and pulls me closer and I say with a quiver to my voice, "That's not fair."

"Good."

He transfers his attention to my lips and kisses me with a passion that always send my mind spiralling out-of-control and as usual there is nothing else in my world but him. He demands all of my attention when he invades my space. He rules my world and decides my next moments in life and the power he has over me excites me as I lose my mind. Nothing else matters but him and that is exactly how it should be, but then I see Sable's imperious expression in my mind as she observes the chaos before her and I groan and push him away.

"I can't."

"Why, this can wait, we can all work together like a team, it's always worked for me?"

Taking deep breaths to regain my mind, I say sadly, "We're not all as well trained as you are. You may think we work as a team but when you've got the team from National Lampoon, think again. Nan and grandad Adams never make it downstairs before eleven. Mum and dad will interfere and argue and nothing will get done before they fall out and storm off in a mood. Your parents will probably help but will need to be monitored and placed on different sides of the building. Heidi would be fine and Harvey I guess, if they can stop flirting long enough to get any actual work done and as for your grandparents, they would distract us far too much with ways to make cleaning fun and probably end up causing more mess in the process."

"So what, it's not as if it matters. Sable and Arthur won't care if it's a bit messy."

Staring at him in horror, I say in shock, "Have you forgotten who's coming? Sable Evans is a woman who doesn't tolerate anything out of place. She is a machine and doesn't appreciate anything less than perfection and this castle is half hers. I'm surprised at you, Finn because you know the importance of having things ship shape and orderly. When you are fighting a war, you can't leave anything to chance. This place has to pass the scrutiny of the most demanding general and I would feel as if I've failed if the place isn't looking its best. No, I'm sorry but everything else will have to be put on hold until it is because I am hyperventilating at the thought that Sable will find me lacking."

Sighing heavily, Finn pulls away and says in a slightly annoyed voice, "Fine. Tell me what to do because even I can see you would only have half a mind on me, anyway."

Brushing off my disappointment, I say briskly, "Ok, you can start clearing all the rubbish and take it to the bins. I'll start washing and when you've finished, you can dry the dishes. Breakfast will have to be a help yourself affair this morning because I have no time to wait on our guests."

Finn shrugs and I can tell he's annoyed but he'll have to suck it up because nothing is going to get in the way of my perfect welcome to Sable and Arthur, not to mention my brother and his plus one.

Trying hard to push down my irritation, I try to
block out the slightly unruly line-up that has
congregated on the edge of the veranda as we wait
for Sable's helicopter to land that is currently
circling above. I am so cross with all of them
because aside from Finn, absolutely nobody saw the
importance of getting the work done. Luckily, with
a superhuman effort on our part, the castle is
looking at its finest and I even managed to throw on
my favourite Stella McCartney sundress that was a
steal from TK Maxx online. To everyone else I look
the picture of organisation and domestic bliss. The
sort of person who could run a blog on living your
best life and be the envy of housewives everywhere.
By my side is the perfect man and our Instagram
feed would go viral if he just allowed me to post
one photograph of him on it. However, Finn isn't
one for publicity because he's lived in the shadows
for far too long in his covert operations when he
worked in the SAS.

Heidi stands sheepishly beside me and I can't
even look at her right now because it turns out she
spent the night in Harvey's gîte and I suppose it was
always going to happen but I thought she was better
than that. Harvey is looking extremely pleased with
himself and well he might because Heidi has
definitely let the side down on this occasion. The
fact that I spent the night with Finn on the first night

we met is irrelevant because in our case, it was a question of survival and I will never admit to it being any different. We were camping at the time and I was in need of warmth that only he could provide, so he did in fact save my life that night.

The nans are chatting as usual and I sigh when I see Stella glaring daggers at Piers who is chatting to my mum at the opposite end of the line-up, totally oblivious to her anger. Dad is regaling Harvey about the joys of golf and none of them look as if they have a care in the world, unlike me whose nerves are frazzled because Sable is circling us like a vulture as we speak and I am anxious not to be found lacking.

Finn reaches for my hand and squeezes it, saying softly, "You look beautiful, Lily. The castle looks amazing and you can relax."

"I won't relax until this wedding is over, Finn because it has to be perfect in every way. I can't leave anything to chance because one thing out of line will spoil it forever."

He sighs and I know he doesn't understand the importance of the finer details. Men don't. They think everything happens on autopilot and don't appreciate the work involved in making something look seamless. They don't appreciate the hours of planning and meticulous execution involved, but Sable does. She knows exactly what I mean and as the helicopter touches down, I have to fight back the tears because despite everything, I am looking forward to seeing her so much. She is everything to me and her approval is all I want because if Sable approves, it means I have done things right and that, at the moment, means more to me than anything.

As the rotor blades slow down, Finn springs forward and goes to help our guests disembark and mum says loudly, "How the other half live. You know, I always wanted a ride in a helicopter, do you think they'll oblige?"

"Ooh yes, we could all take it in turns. Maybe they can fly us around the Eiffel tower with a glass of champagne in our hands."

Nan sounds excited and I say sharply, "There will be no joyriding in helicopters. No, I expect he has a strict schedule to adhere to and these things cost money."

Taking a few deep calming breaths, I focus on watching the woman herself exit the helicopter and take the helping hand Finn offers her.

"I like her dress, looks like Chanel."

Stella suddenly looks more animated than she has since she arrived and I nod, "Yes, Sable is very stylish and the Chanel is the perfect choice when visiting France. You know, she is such a considerate woman, showcasing French fashion as a nod to their superiority when it comes to chic and effortless fashion choices."

Heidi bursts out laughing and I stare at her because she has no right to comment. Heidi's fashion choices usually involved knitted items that she has made herself, and no amount of convincing me will ever make me see her as anything but bohemian. The fact she is wearing a very pretty chiffon light blue sundress today is not important because it's what she usually wears that counts. In fact, the more I look at her, the more different she looks. I note the blush to her cheeks and the sparkle in her eyes. Her hair is long and glossy and looks newly washed and styled with rollers, giving her loose curls that make her look pretty and stylish. She is wearing silver sandals and her nails are painted in a pretty pink and I wonder how I missed this total transformation. Gone is the hunched figure of the broken girl who arrived not long ago with a haunted expression in her eyes. In its place is a woman blossoming in the sunshine. She looks so happy and nothing like a woman who is grieving for the loss of the love of her life and standing beside her is obviously the reason because the heat coming off the two of them is hotter than the sun on our backs as I watch them share a look loaded with so much fire, I feel the burn from here.

Dragging my attention away, I stand a little straighter as I watch the procession heading towards us. Sable, as expected, leads the charge, closely followed by Arthur who is helping Finn with the bags. Behind them are Sybil and Stacey, Sable's assistants and as I see them walking towards me, I breathe a sigh of relief. Thank God they are here and now every problem that presents itself will be dealt with effortlessly by the woman in charge.

Stepping forward, I smile brightly and kiss Sable three times.

"Welcome, how was your journey?"

"A little fractious if I'm honest. The pilot forgot to pick up the champagne that's vital to a trip like this and consequently we had zero refreshment to get us through."

Nodding towards the silver tray set up on the nearby table dressed with a starched white tablecloth, I smile. "Then please let me offer you the finest champagne, or a welcome Pimm's cocktail."

"Darling, you're a lifesaver, I knew I could count on you, Lily, darling. You are my lighthouse in a raging storm."

She reaches over and grabs one of the glasses and looks around her with interest as I proceed to walk her up the welcoming line introducing everyone. I look at my nan in astonishment as she curtseys and says politely, "Your majesty."

Mum rolls her eyes and smiles at Sable. "Don't mind her, she's a little confused."

Watching Sable surrounded by my family is a strange experience. It's as if my two worlds have collided and it's a very strange sight. Suddenly, my attention is diverted when I hear, "So here she is, the blushing bride."

Turning, I see Arthur, Sable's husband beaming beside Finn and I step into his outstretched arms as he whispers, "You look beautiful, Lily. The castle looks amazing and we can't wait to see the results of all your hard labour."

103

As I hug him back, my heart lifts. Arthur is such a great guy and is the constant in Sable's crazy world. He tolerates so much from her and yet does so with an authority that always fascinates me because around him, she is a different person. She loses her hard edge and defers to him on just about everything. For a confident woman in the workplace, she is completely different with him and it makes her appear almost human. Yes, Sable needs this amazing man because he keeps her real and so I hug him back and say happily, "I'm so glad you're here."

"Wouldn't miss it for the world, darling."

He moves on to say hi to the others and I focus on Sybil and Stacey who are looking around them with awe. Sybil has been Sable's assistant for as long as I've known her and Stacey became the deputy editor of Designer Homes - *on a budget* when my predecessor Joseph Maltravers jumped ship and went to The Horse and Hound as deputy editor. None of us were sorry to see him go because he was the sort of person who got where he was off the back of everyone else's ideas, so it was no surprise he left after Sable made things difficult for him when she returned from France after a disastrous change of career. Finn and I swapped places with her and we have never looked back. Now the months and years of all our hard work is about to be tested and I am anxious that everything goes well.

Stacey steps forward and smiles. "Lily, you look lovely and I am blown away by this place. You are living like a queen."

"Thanks, you're looking good yourself." Stacey blushes and looks pleased, but I meant every word. She always was a pretty girl but now, after settling into her new role, she has really blossomed. She is wearing a cream silk lounge suit and has beautiful silver jewellery on her wrists and around her neck. Her blonde curls are pulled back in a stylish ponytail and she is wearing oversized sunglasses that just accentuate the small delicate features of a pretty face. She looks fragile and yet so incredibly chic, it brings out my protective instinct and I hug her warmly. Turning to Sybil, I fight back the tears because this woman has helped me so much over the years. Nothing is too much for her and anything I ask for is done without question and quickly and efficiently. Sybil is also wasted as an assistant because Victoria Secrets are obviously missing an Angel. She is a typical blonde bombshell that wouldn't look out of place on a beach in California and I was always interested to hear the details of the many dates she had lined up when I was her boss. She looks pleased to see me and hugs me tightly, whispering, "I've missed you, darling."

Feeling quite emotional, I nod and say through my tears, "Same."

The thing is, I have missed them. I've missed the excitement working at a magazine brings. The deadlines, the thrill of seeing my ideas in print and the hustle and bustle of London. Living in Provence is everything but I still crave the excitement of my past and then as I see Finn smiling at me from across the veranda, once again, nothing else matters but him. All the turmoil of earlier is forgotten in an instant as I reconnect with the reason we're here at all. Finn and Lily, two people in love who are making the ultimate commitment and I feel ashamed that all of this got in the way of the most important thing in all of this. Him.

♥ *14*

I feel a little nervous as I sit opposite Sable in the office Finn and I use to run the business end of the castle. Typically, Sable is sitting in my usual chair and I'm opposite in the one reserved for visitors. It's just the two of us after showing the new arrivals around the castle and leaving them to settle in.

I was so nervous showing Sable and Arthur around their investment and looked anxiously for any signs of approval, but as usual she kept her cards extremely close to her chest.

Now it's just the two of us and I know I may not like what I'm about to hear, so I take a deep breath and dig my nails into the palm of my hand to keep myself focused on the wise words that usually spill from her lips.

"You have impressed me, darling."

I breathe out – a little.

"The Castle of Dreams is coming along well and you have worked a miracle with the interior."

I feel myself relax and yet sit straight and slightly forward to hang onto her every word.

"As I'm sure you're aware, darling, I brought Stacey along for a reason."

I nod and she taps her perfect nails on the desk. "Your wedding will be featured in the summer issue of Designer Homes - *on a budget*. We will run editorial content and print before and after photographs of the castle's transformation. There will be a link to the castle's website and a special

107

offer to our readers to encourage bookings. Stacey will take care of the feature and Sybil is here to assist her. Gerome is on his way and will take care of the photographs."

Feeling a little worried, I say anxiously, "Gerome? I'm sorry, Sable, I'm not sure if I have a spare room."

Waving my question away, she says firmly, "He will commute from the hotel in town. He will also be your wedding photographer and I have negotiated those on a free basis."

Holding her hand up, she says smugly, "Don't thank me, darling. He will have the use of them for his portfolio, so he is more than happy. I mean, with your looks and Finn's, he would pay top dollar to secure such a couple from a modelling agency. Now, we need to touch base on the arrangements."

A sick feeling washes over me as I think about Gerome and his portfolio. Ordinarily it would be ok but Finn is extremely camera shy and certainly will not agree to his image being used commercially and then there's my dress. Just thinking of the world seeing me dressed like Pollyanna in my nan's aged wedding dress is making me have palpitations. If it was the Givenchy, well, that would be another matter but just thinking about the look in Sable's eye as I tell her the bad news, makes me want to go for a lie down.

She doesn't appear to notice that the blood has drained from my face as she produces her large A5 leather-bound notebook that she keeps all her lists and meeting notes in and turns to a page that is full of lists and ticks already.

"Right then, photographer sorted and gratis. Best man present and correct."

She looks at me sharply, "Have the rings arrived?"

"I think so."

Looking annoyed, she circles the bullet point in her notebook and mumbles, "I will address that issue in my meeting with the groom and best man."

Consulting her list again, she says, "Entertainment. Yes, I've booked a local band to provide soft music throughout the ceremony and meal, followed by a disco in the evening. I'm sure you'll approve; they have also agreed to provide their services free on the proviso we recommend them to our future brides and grooms and provide a listing in the wedding portfolio we send out."

Wow, Sable is on it and I look at her with complete adoration.

"Ok, caterers are booked and have agreed we only need to cover their costs. They are offering us their service free for the same deal. Flowers, same, from the local florists and they are throwing in a wedding arch decorated with daisies as requested."

I fight back the tears at the mention of it because I can't bear to think that my Aunt Daisy won't be here to see me marry the man of my dreams. It was down to her that I met Finn in the first place when I was carrying out her bucket list after she died. It was her one regret in life that she never found love and I wish more than anything that she could see me now.

As I brush a tear away, Sable snaps, "No time for sentiment, Lily, we need to press on."

"Ok, the cake is being delivered on the day from a reputable bakery on the same deal as before."

She looks up and I see her eyes shine as she smiles with satisfaction. "You know, this wedding has been a godsend because everyone was falling over themselves to provide their services in return for a mention in our portfolio. I really think we have nailed this, Lily and will have our photographs and contact list ready to go by the end of the month."

Looking down, she begins listing the remainder of the items on her list.

"Ok, I have a beautician and hairdresser arriving at 9 am on the day. They will set up in the music room and operate on a tight schedule. Anyone wishing to avail themselves of their services needs to book an appointment with Sybil, who is running the diary. However, you my darling, along with Heidi and myself are booked in at 10 am at intervals of 30 minutes apart. Obviously, I will go first because I need to be on hand to organise the celebrations and make sure things are running smoothly. Now, tell me, have the dresses arrived?"

I actually squirm as she fixes me with her razor-sharp stare and say in a small voice, "Um... about that."

She looks at me keenly and I laugh nervously. "Um... the bridesmaids dresses are being delivered this afternoon and my nan is currently caring for my wedding dress."

"Good, I will look forward to seeing it later."

I feel sick as I shake my head. "It's um… not quite what I had planned but was the best on offer at the time."

"Ok, what's the problem?"

Sable leans forward and I see the hunger in her eyes stripping me bare as she senses a problem she can pounce on. Wearily, I fill her in and she stares at me in astonishment. "Oh no, Lily, that just won't do at all. Give me the dress shop details and I will arrange the delivery of your dress this afternoon."

"But they're closed, there's nobody there."

Sable looks astounded. "There must be someone we can call. As I said, leave it with me, darling, I will make it my number one priority."

"But my nan, she's set her heart on me wearing her dress."

Sable sighs with exasperation and fixes me with a look that could curdle milk.

"This is not your nan's day, Lily, it's yours and Finn's. Now I know you want to please everyone, but that doesn't work if you don't please yourself in the process. Your nan will understand, after all, she's a woman and we understand everything. No, leave it with me and I will solve the problem of the wedding dress. Now, Arthur has arranged the men's suits, so we can tick that one off at least, he picked them up from Savile row and we have brought them with us."

I open my mouth to speak and she holds up her hand. "Don't thank me, darling, it's our contribution. After all, Finn is family."

Lowering her voice, she leans forward. "How are things between Aunt Stella and Uncle Piers? I'm guessing things are a little awkward."

Nodding miserably, I sigh. "It doesn't look good."

"Hmm, he always was a scoundrel. Maybe we can find her a new man, someone with a good dose of moral decency and a satisfying sex drive."

"Sable!" I giggle because I don't think I've ever heard Sable refer to sex at all and it seems strange. She smiles and says in a whisper, "It's a well-known fact that the male libido lessens as a woman's increases. Piers won't be able to keep it up for long and Stella will thank us in the long run while she is being entertained by a younger stud. I'm guessing Piers won't be so pleased with himself then."

She laughs and then looks back at her notebook.

"To be honest, Lily, this list is so long we could be here until morning. Do you trust me to have taken care of everything because I'm happy to continue if you are?"

Feeling relieved to be let off the hook, I nod like an obedient puppy. "Of course, I trust you implicitly."

"Good, then we will wrap this up and go and join the others. I need to freshen up anyway and quite frankly, I haven't seen Arthur much over the past few weeks so we have some catching up to do as a matter of urgency."

She winks as she snaps her notebook shut, leaving me reeling and just a little disturbed. It's only 2.20 in the afternoon and they've been married for ages. Surely they can wait.

However, apparently not because as we leave the sanctuary of the office, Arthur is waiting and on seeing us approach, I watch his expression change as he focuses solely on his wife and from the look in his eye, they are not to be disturbed.

♥ *15*

Somehow Finn and I have managed to escape the crowd and are taking a leisurely stroll around the lake that sparkles like a jewel behind the castle. It's one of my favourite places to go and think and I take a deep breath of pure oxygen. Finn's arm is slung around my shoulders and it's just the two of us as it usually is and I feel as if I can breathe again.

Finn is as relaxed as always but I am turning into a nervous wreck and now that Sable is here, I can slack off a little because I know she will have everything covered.

"This is nice."

Finn seems happy and I nod in agreement. "It is, in fact, it's come at the right time because I was getting seriously stressed out by everything that's going on."

Pulling me down on the grassy bank, Finn rolls on his back and pulls me into his side and I lay my head on his chest as he strokes my hair with his fingers.

He whispers, "None of that matters, Adams. I would marry you in a field with only the cows for company if it meant you became my wife. The rest is irrelevant as far as I'm concerned."

My heart almost bursts with love for him as I feel a little foolish at how obsessed I've been over the last few days.

"I'm sorry, Finn." My voice is but a whisper and he turns to look at me in surprise. "For what?"

"For forgetting what this is all about. I've been self-obsessed and moody and haven't made time for *us*. All I could think about was making everything perfect and this, lying here with you, is all the perfection I need."

The look Finn gives me washes away any worries I had as he kisses me so softly, I think of nothing else. The birds sing overhead and the sun warms our skin as we kiss like the lovers we are on the edge of the cool crystal lake. Maybe it's because we love each other, or maybe it's because of the romantic setting but passion fans the flames and we get a little carried away and go just a bit too far and are soon making passionate love by the water's edge. Sex with Finn is always great, but this is off the charts and I am oblivious to anything but him. So, it's with considerable anxiety that as we readjust our clothing, I see the glint of something in the trees and whisper, "What's that?"

"What?"

"Over there, there's something in those trees. Oh my god, do you think it's a stray photographer taking pot shots, or a trespasser? Oh, my goodness, what if there's a prowler on the loose, we could be in danger, this is a disaster?"

Finn laughs. "Why would he be interested in us? We're hardly celebrities."

"Please, Finn, what if it's one of the guests, this won't look good in the wedding album? I could never look my family in the eye again."

Finn starts laughing and I say crossly, "You're the special forces guy, go and do something, um… special."

"I thought I just did."

He laughs even harder and I say crossly, "Fine, but don't blame me if we're outed at the reception. I bet it's Harvey playing a prank on us and quite frankly, if I see one photograph of that, it will ruin my life."

"You're a little melodramatic, aren't you?"

"Says you."

"Why me, I'm the least dramatic person I know?"

"True but I couldn't think of anything else to say."

We grin at each other and he reaches across and pulls me towards him, saying softly, "Relax. If it was anyone, they're so far away they wouldn't have seen a thing. Anyway, it doesn't bother me at all. The only thing that does is you and if I want to show you how much you mean to me then I will, over and over again."

Once again, he kisses me so sweetly I instantly forget about the prowler. If there is one, he would be a fool because we have the SAS in residence and our safety is guaranteed.

We make our way back to the Castle of Dreams, hoping that everyone is happy and has what they want. I never realised what would be involved in entertaining so many people at once and it worries me a little for our future. If I'm struggling now, what will it be like when we have paying guests? Thank goodness I asked Heidi to help out. At least she will provide a willing pair of hands when I need them.

I know we will have to recruit more staff and I have put an ad in the window of the store in town but it's starting to worry me about the enormity of the task ahead of me.

However, as we make our way towards the castle, I am met by an extremely worried looking mother who says in a slightly high voice, "Um... Lily darling, your last guests have arrived."

I share a look with Finn and can't stop the smile from breaking as I say happily, "Is Mark here already?"

"Yes, darling and Kylie."

"Ooh what's she like? Does she look like the real Kylie?"

Finn snorts. "I'm pretty sure in her eyes she *is* the real Kylie."

"Oh, you know what I mean. So, tell me mum, is she small and petite with strawberry blonde hair? Does she have a really cute Australian accent and is she wearing a hat with corks strung around it? Oh, my goodness, just think of the conversations we will have about neighbours and who's her favourite character, you know, she may even know then personally, this is too much, I'm hyperventilating with excitement."

Finn laughs and places his hand firmly around my mouth and says firmly, "Stop talking, Adams, you're making no sense. Calm down and we'll go and welcome your brother and his girlfriend without the twenty questions."

We head inside and I can tell mum is stewing on something, so pull her to a stop and nod to Finn to head in without us. As soon as he leaves, I say firmly, "Ok, what's up?"

"I'm just being silly."

"I'll be the judge of that, go on, what's wrong?"

Sighing, she sits on the nearby bench and pulls me beside her, looking anxious. "I don't know really but she is a little odd if I'm honest."

"In what way?"

"Well, she's nothing like I expected and is very forceful. She's also tall, I mean, Mark is tall but Kylie is an amazon. She is just different and totally unexpected."

"What does nan think of her?"

"I could tell she was a little taken aback. We all were if I'm honest but you can form your own opinion and then let me know if you can put your finger on it."

It surprises me that mum is out here at all and not monopolising Mark's time because she's missed him so much and talked of little else but his return, so I know something must be very wrong.

"So, where are they now?"

"With the others in the kitchen, helping themselves to lunch."

"Well, come on then, I can't wait to meet them."

As I stand to leave, mum pulls me back and says anxiously, "You do think it will be ok, don't you?"

"What?"

"Mark, the wedding, oh everything really?"

"What makes you ask?"

"I don't know. I've just got a feeling that something bad is going to happen and it reminds me of the legend of the Chateau du Reves."

"Not that again, honestly, I thought we had finished with that."

"You may have but I've thought of nothing else. You know, I'm convinced that poor couple's ghosts haunt this place. I hear them groaning at night and it's quite eerie, really."

Feeling my face blush a deep shade of red, I wonder how thick these walls are. Mum and dad are in the room opposite ours and I hope it wasn't us she heard. We can be a little vocal when we go to bed and I'd hate to think my parents hear us."

"Rubbish, of course this place isn't haunted, whatever next?"

I turn away before she sees my face burning and puts two and two together but she says darkly, "I know what I heard and it was definitely wailing. You know it wouldn't surprise me if they're watching us now from the turret."

"Mum, please stop. I've lived here for two years and heard nothing, why would they be here now?"

"Because of the wedding, Lily. It has brought the legend to life again and it promises devastation."

"Oh, for goodness' sake get a grip and let's go and see what all the fuss is about."

My earlier glow has now firmly vanished as I stomp inside the castle to find the others. Haunted indeed, whatever next?

♥ 16

The first person I see when I head into the kitchen is Kylie. It's hard to miss her because she is, as mum suggested, an Amazonian. Extremely tall, very athletic looking, with short dark hair that is more practical than styled and eyes that zone in on you the moment you look in her general direction. She's also way older than Mark, which is why I expect my mums so concerned. I catch my breath as I see him holding onto her arm and then shake myself as I contemplate my brother. He's changed. Really changed. I suppose I must have too because after three years a person can change a lot. Even though we kept in touch on Skype, I didn't register how much weight he's lost. He looks toned and in the peak of condition and his long messy hair has been cut short, making him look as if he's in the military. Gone are the scruffy jeans and t-shirts and in their place are smart chinos and a button-down shirt. He looks happy to see me though and instinctively I run towards him and feel slightly concerned that he looks at Kylie first before she nods and he drops his arm from hers and envelops me in a big hug.

"I've missed you so much." I almost can't get the words out because it's true. It's only after seeing him here in front of me that it sinks in how much I have indeed missed him. He may be my annoying little brother, but he's not so little anymore and is actually only two years younger than me.

"Good to see you, sis, I've missed you too."

He pulls away and smiles, but I see an edge in his eyes that never used to be there before. A sort of wariness that means he's not entirely comfortable and then he turns and says softly, "Kylie, this is my sister, Lily."

"Pleased to meet you, Lily."

She stares at Mark pointedly and he returns to her side and takes her hand in his and I don't miss the barely disguised smirk on Finn's face as he catches my eye.

Feeling a little out of sorts, I shake myself and say brightly, "Well, isn't this nice. You must be exhausted after that humongous journey. Why don't you let me show you to your room?"

"No need, we have already unpacked."

Kylie is abrupt and nods towards mum. "Sonia showed us and David helped Mark with the bags. So, this is what passes for a castle these days, is it?"

She looks around her dismissively and I try not to let it but her comment pierces my heart. Mum steps forward and says loudly, "Come, let's take our lunch onto the veranda, I want to hear all about you."

Kylie shrugs and I watch in disbelief as Mark picks up two plates of food and some cutlery for both of them and follows them out, Kylie striding empty handed in front of him.

I stare at Finn in shock who appears to be sharing a private joke with Harvey and then I see nan and granddad looking as shocked as I am and whisper, "What do you make of her?"

"Not a lot if I'm honest, darling." Nan never holds back and shakes her head. "She's a strange one, that's for sure. Maybe she's shy."

Grandad snorts loudly. "I think she's anything but shy. God help Mark though; he's got himself a weird one there."

Feeling annoyed for Mark, I start to defend him and then Stella and Piers come in, followed by her parents.

"Room for four more."

Betty manages to diffuse an awkward conversation and I set about helping them fill their plates before directing them outside.

The others follow and soon it's only Heidi and me and I say in shock, "What do you make of, Kylie?"

"She's a bitch."

"Heidi, that's a bit unkind."

"I say it how it is. Poor Mark, you should have seen her when they arrived. He was falling over his feet to please her and she didn't even lift a finger. If you ask me, he's so under her thumb it's not healthy."

"Did you think she was a little um… manly?"

Heidi giggles. "And then some. She looks more manly than Mark and that's saying something."

I stare at her sharply and she grins and looks away. Reaching for a couple of bottles of wine, she sighs. "Anyway, we should head outside. I think the others are already there. You know, this is exhausting, Lily, there are so many people here you will soon have to have sittings."

As I follow her out, I'm beginning to think I've bitten off more than I can chew. She's right, this is getting out of control.

By the time Sable and her entourage join us, I am having multiple panic attacks. I can't cope, it's too much, all of these people in one place demanding things. If I thought my family would help out, I was sorely mistaken because they appear to have settled into holiday mode and don't seem to think they need to lift a finger to help. Finn is enjoying spending time with Harvey, which I completely understand because they rarely see each other. I feel the same about Heidi but feel a little happier knowing she will be living here soon.

It's only when Sable fixes me with the look that means business, I know something is about to change.

Nodding towards the castle, she stands and I follow like the dutiful worshipper I always have been.

She leads me to the office and points to the chair opposite my usual one and then sits before me, making me feel as if I'm in the headmistress's study.

"Lily, this can't go on."

"What can't go on?"

I feel my anxiety reaching a new level as I wonder what part of this chaos can't go on and she sighs irritably.

"This fiasco. There are far too many people here and you are struggling. This is meant to be your special event and you are running around in circles and will soon burn out. I am here to shoulder the burden and thought I had already done so with organising the wedding but this – circus." She stops and stares at me with a steely glint in her eye, "Stops now."

I stare at her in astonishment as she stands and starts pacing around the room like she used to do in her glass office in London.

"I will have to take steps to organise your family. From now on, you are to sit back and do nothing. I will not have my bride an emotional and physical wreck on her wedding day. So, to show I mean business, you are to be dropped off at the local spa retreat this afternoon with Heidi as company. I have arranged the full package for you both, including a massage with a very experienced masseuse along with facials and mani-pedis. I do not, repeat, do not want to see you until tomorrow morning."

"Tomorrow!"

I stare at her in shock and she nods with the look on her face that means nothing I say will change a thing.

"But isn't it rude for me to leave my guests, what about Mark and Kylie, they've only just arrived?"

A flicker of distaste passes across her face and she sneers. "You leave that woman to me."

"Don't you like her?"

Suddenly I'm interested because Sable is a good judge of character and can analyse a person within minutes of meeting them.

"Let's just say I have my suspicions and leave it at that."

"Suspicions!" Immediately my mind is awash with images of a pantomime villain. Obviously Sable has seen something in Kylie she doesn't like and I wonder what it could be. Mum also had the same look on her face and I know, before I go anywhere, I will have to find out what they're thinking, starting with my mum.

Sable nods and then her expression softens, which totally transforms her face. She is a beautiful woman but always a little fierce. However, now she has a softness to her that is captivating and I feel myself willing to do absolutely anything she tells me to. "So, darling, you head off and pack your overnight bag. Say your goodbyes to Finn and your family because the taxi is booked for 2.30 sharp."

"But that's in half an hour."

"Then you had better get moving."

She smiles and for a moment I am lost for words and then the relief hits me. I'm off the hook. Finally, I can relax and leave the chaos behind and I owe it all to the woman in front of me like I always do. She has always had my back and this is no exception.

Feeling the tears building, I make to speak and she raises her hand. "Don't thank me, darling. It was a necessary step. Now go and make sure you have an amazing time."

As I walk out of the office, I feel so blessed to have Sable in my life. The best friend a woman could ever have because she always sees the approaching storm coming and diverts you away from the devastation it causes. Then I feel the excitement building for a sneaky night away. This is too good to be true and I get to experience it with my best friend. What could be better than this?

I'm in shock. In fact, I still can't believe what just happened.

As the car moves away from the castle, I stare at the waving hands of my entire family and say to Heidi, "This is unbelievable."

Laughing, she sits back and stretches with contentment.

"I could get used to this."

Leaning over, she grabs a bottle nestling in the cooler and pours me a glass of champagne and one for herself. "You know, Lily, I could get used to this lifestyle. I'll say one thing for Sable, she has class."

I stare around at the luxurious limo that she arranged to pick us up and feel so happy I could burst. I can't believe she did this for me, it's too much.

Heidi sips the champagne and giggles. "Did you see the look on Kylie's face, she was so jealous."

"What do you think about her? I mean, mum said she's peculiar."

"And the rest."

"Did you speak to her, what's she like?"

"I told you, she's a bitch." Heidi turns and I see a wicked glint in her eye. "You know, I heard her telling Mark off terribly when she thought they were alone."

"What did she say?" I feel angry on behalf of my brother and Heidi shrugs. "Apparently, he hadn't topped her drink up when it was empty and she was raging."

"That's ridiculous."

"I know."

"What did Mark say?" I feel curious as to what my brother would say to her and Heidi laughs softly. "He just apologised and told her it wouldn't happen again."

I don't like the sound of this at all and sit silently fuming. Then Heidi laughs. "Harvey told me some guys like that sort of thing. She may be like a mother figure to him and that's the appeal."

"Eew, that's disgusting, Mark's not a weirdo."

"No, I don't think he is." Heidi looks away and something about her expression tells me she knows something I don't.

"So, tell me about Harvey, what's happening there?"

She turns and grins and her eyes sparkle with excitement which makes my heart sink. Just great.

"He is just what I need right now. You know, I really think he was sent from God to help me out in a crisis. I can't believe my luck because I haven't had so much fun in ages."

"Um... when you say fun, what does that mean exactly?"

I almost dread her reply and the way her cheeks turn pink and her eyes sparkle, I already know the answer to my question. "Well, you can't blame a girl for indulging, can you? I'd be a fool to pass that opportunity by."

I'm not sure it's my place to but I feel as if I should warn her. "You do know he's not likely to stick around for long, don't you?"

I feel a little anxious because the last thing I want is for Heidi to get her hopes up and fall in love with the rogue.

"I guess. He did say he was due back to work at the end of next week. He wouldn't tell me what though, or where. It kind of adds to the mystery and is such a turn on."

Thinking back to how secretive Finn always was on what he did for a living, I know what she means. There's something so incredibly powerful about a man of mystery and I know that Heidi is already a lost cause. Shifting the conversation, I say a little too brightly, "And Thomas, have you heard from him?"

"Nope."

Her answer is short and abrupt and her expression tells me she doesn't even want to *think* about him and I feel bad for her.

Taking a sip of the cool sparkling liquid, I think about the snatched conversation I had with my mum while I was packing. She was worried and told me something was very wrong with Mark. She said she was going to make it her motherly mission to get to the bottom of it and her biggest fear is that he's involved with a cult.

Feeling anxious, I turn to Heidi and blurt out, "Do you think Mark's in a cult?"

She almost chokes on her drink and laughs loudly, "Are you serious?"

"Mum is. She told me something is definitely up with Mark and that Kylie woman and she fears he's become indoctrinated in a cult. Have you ever had any experience of one?"

"Why would I?" Heidi laughs fit to burst and I feel a little annoyed because I'm deadly serious.

"It's no laughing matter, Heidi, you hear of it all the time."

"No, you don't."

"Well, you do if you google it. It happens a lot you know and goes on in even the most suburban areas, my mum told me."

Heidi looks interested. "Your mum is such an interesting woman, Lily. Firstly, I've never met anyone who knows as much as she does about Midsommer murders. I mean, it's impressive and she should really consider going on mastermind with that as her specialist subject."

"Don't encourage her." I groan out loud and Heidi shakes her head. "Go on, what has she found out?"

"Apparently, they have them in Australia too and they are scary places to be. Mum's worried because she heard terrible things, well, read an article on it in the Sydney times, actually."

"What did it say?"

Heidi's eyes are wide and I say with concern. "Apparently, the women in the cult are in charge and the men are their slaves. Sound familiar?"

Now Heidi's face mirrors my own and she gasps, "That's terrible."

"Yes, because these women are brutal, apparently. The men are treated like dogs and there only to worship the women. If they are displeased, then they are punished."

"Ooh, how?"

"Well, mum told me, in a very worried voice I might add, that there were reports of a murder there last year."

"Of course, there was?"

Heidi rolls her eyes and I have to laugh. "Well, yes, that would have kept mum's interest that's for sure, anyway, the police were called and reported a very strange set up. The women were hard and cool and the men like robots. When questioned, they all said the same thing."

"Which was?"

"That they were happy and fulfilled and there was nothing to be concerned about. There was no evidence of anything else, so the police had to leave. However, there was also a report in the same article that one of the men had escaped and told a story that was so horrific he had to have therapy for the rest of his life."

"What was it?"

"I don't know, she said she had been interrupted and was going to do some more digging later this evening."

"Wow, that's some story. I would love to know more."

"Me too. Do you think Mark's involved in it?"

Heidi now looks as worried as I do and whispers, "Possibly, do you think we should report her to the police and they could look into it?"

"Maybe not this time but if my mums on the case, we should know everything the minute we return to the castle."

By the time we reach the Spa de Provence, we have run through every reason why Mark likes Kylie and none of them seem convincing.

Trying to put it out of my mind, I look in awe at the beautiful building we pull up outside and feel the waves of relaxation washing over me. We're here.

♥ 18

It feels as if we can't speak. The atmosphere is so serene I wonder if we've been sent to a convent. All around us is polished marble and the smell is utterly divine. A calming mix of sandalwood and lemon with some kind of spice thrown in. Just what the doctor ordered.

A very polished receptionist dressed in a black uniform smiles and says in perfect English. "Welcome to the Spa de Provence. Please take a seat and someone will be with you shortly."

We perch on the edge of a luxurious sofa in the reception area and Heidi almost can't contain her excitement.

She whispers, "I could live here."

"It's certainly impressive."

Quickly, I whip out my phone and say in a whisper, "Let's grab a shot for Instagram and add it to my 'Living my best life' story. I'm sure to get a few new followers with this one, this place is the stuff of dreams."

Heidi nods in agreement and we pose for the camera, making sure to add my favourite filter because nothing is at it seems on Instagram, after all.

By the time I've added my usual twenty hashtags, I'm aware that someone's coming.

I watch with interest as a woman dressed in the same black uniform approaches us and smiles before handing us both a hot towel. "Welcome, please refresh yourselves with a hot towel and then fill in your details while I fetch you a welcome invigorating juice."

Feeling the warm steam instantly calm my frayed nerves, I silently thank Sable from the bottom of my heart. How did she know this was just what I needed?

The lady hands us a clipboard each and heads off, and Heidi starts scribbling immediately. I follow and it's just the usual information like name, address etc and health questionnaire and the woman returns and hands us both a glass of a weird looking green juice.

"This is an invigorating rejuvenating juice to restore your body's imbalance. It contains Chai seeds, almond milk, green apple, avocado and lemon."

Heidi shrugs and drinks the liquid in one go and then shivers. "Wow."

She grins and I rise to the challenge in her eyes and do the same and feel the punch of health work its way to my core. Wow indeed.

The woman nods and says brightly, "Please follow me and I will explain everything."

Feeling a little lightheaded, we follow her through the reception area as she proceeds to give us a tour of the building. There are treatment rooms, a gym and a sauna. She points out an indoor swimming pool and then takes us outside where there are two further pools with loungers set around them with huge white cushions welcoming you to luxury. The pool nearest the building is heated to 35 degrees all year round and has sunbeds built in, allowing you to rest in luxury with the warmth bathing your body in comfort. The second pool is a natural one that has been infused with minerals to aid the body's healing and recovery process.

Heidi whispers, "I don't think I fancy going under in that pool, it's as green as that drink."

"Maybe that's where the drink came from."

I laugh as she pulls a face looking a little green herself before we are shown to the changing room where we find a white robe and slippers waiting for us in our assigned locker.

"Now, ladies, your first treatment is at 4 o'clock, so please relax and use the facilities first. Then make your way to treatment room 4 where the masseurs will be waiting for you."

She leaves us to it and I can't change quickly enough. This is the best day ever and I get to share it with my closest friend.

We spend the next hour relaxing by the hot pool and alternating between the two. There is also a jacuzzi nearby with brightly coloured juices to sip in plastic glasses while we unwind and let go of the troubles we had to agree to leave at the door.

Neither of us speak much because this place frowns upon noise and to be honest, it's the perfect place to unwind and close off our minds for a much-needed recharge.

Just before 4pm we head to room 4 and I wonder what we'll find.

Heidi knocks gently and we hear a soft, "Enter."

As we head inside, the room is almost in darkness and only the scented candles flicker in the dim light. It smells amazing and as I breathe deeply, I take in the scent of eucalyptus oil and lemon which clears my nasal passages and de-stresses my mind.

Then I take a second look because waiting for us are two men that look as if they were sent from heaven for our pleasure. Two blond bombshells with muscles that glisten under the oil that is liberally coating their biceps. I daren't even look at Heidi as one of them speaks in a sexy French accent. "Bonjour Mademoiselles Lily et Heidi. Je m'appelle Luis et mon ami et Beau."

I just smile and Heidi stares at them shyly.

They are standing beside two treatment beds that are covered in black towels and Beau smiles at Heidi and says softly, "Mademoiselle, veuillez retirer votre robe et vous allonger sur la table."

"What did he just say?" Heidi whispers and I hiss, "Remove your robe and lie on the table."

"Oh, dear God, my prayers have been answered."

She smiles so brightly I have to laugh as she slips her robe from her shoulders and stands in nothing but her bikini.

I watch as she lays down and then Luis repeats the same instructions to me and I quickly take my place on the table next to her.

We lie face down and then Beau kneels down and says to Heidi, "Nous quitterons la pièce pour que vous puissiez retirer votre haut."

She looks across and I say faintly, "He said, they will leave the room and we must remove our tops."

The look on Heidi's face makes me laugh and I say quickly, "Merci, pas de problème."

The men leave and Heidi says in awe, "Wow, Lily, since when did you speak the lingo?"

"Well, I have lived here for two years already and Finn taught me everything he knows."

Heidi grins. "I bet he did."

Shrugging out of my bikini top, I feel slightly concerned that I will have a gorgeous man's hands roaming all over my body and Heidi laughs softly. "You know, if he had told me to lie back and think of England, I would have done."

"You're shocking."

"I'm sorry, Lily, but you're the one getting married. I'm the single one having experiences with nobody around to judge me. Just think of that particular memory to keep me warm in my old age."

"Well, if you put it like that."

We start giggling and almost don't notice them return until they stand beside the bed and say in a gentle voice.

"Détendez-vous, je vais commencer à vous masser."

I nod and say to Heidi, "They want us to relax, they're starting."

As I try and ignore the fact that a gorgeous man is now manhandling my body, I allow myself to empty my mind. Even the sound of Heidi giggling and squirming beside me doesn't divert my attention from the fact this is the best thing ever. His touch is gentle but firm and as he applies the oils, I breathe in a heavenly scent that makes me relax and lose control of every muscle in my body.

After a while, I hear Heidi groaning and I stifle a giggle. Soft music plays through the speakers that sounds like some form of whale music and it feels as if I'm in a different world.

It must be fifteen minutes later that his hands leave my body and he whispers, "Je vais partir et vous pouvez mettre votre haut avant de masser le devant."

"Merci."

They leave and I whisper, "They want to do the front now."

"Whoa, now you're talking."

"Don't be so rude. You need to put your top on."

"Do I have to?"

Heidi starts giggling and I shake my head as I fumble for my wet bikini top.

Heidi does the same and whispers, "Do you think Beau will come home with me. He has amazing hands."

"That's not the only amazing thing about him."

"You can say that again. Do you think they choose these men on looks because I don't think it would be the same if he wasn't so hot?"

"It shouldn't matter, it's what they do with their hands that count."

"Keep telling yourself that."

She breaks off as the door opens and I close my eyes tightly shut as they return and begin to manhandle my body. Once again Heidi starts to groan and I hope she's not so loud when staying with Harvey because Oscar and Betty are only next door and they would be shocked. Then again, thinking about Finn's grandparents, I push that foolish thought away because I'm sure they are shocked at nothing.

Thirty minutes of pure and unadulterated pleasure later, we are released from our cocoon of pleasure and head back to the pool area to grab another rejuvenating juice and try to wake up from the obvious dream we just experienced.

♥ 19

Two hours later, we are shown to our room and look around with pure happiness. As rooms go, this one is fit for a queen and I gasp as I move to the window and stare across a garden that wouldn't look out of place in a magazine.

The room itself is large and spacious, decorated mainly in white, and everything about it screams relaxation.

Heidi just wanders around in awe and then lies back on one of the two beds that sit side by side and sighs happily. "I'm in heaven on a large white fluffy cloud."

I jump onto the one next to her and have to agree.

In fact, it takes all our will power to leave the comfort of it and dress for dinner. Apparently, we have a three-course healthy meal to enjoy with the obligatory wine.

As we apply our make up in the bathroom, Heidi says, "Those treatments were amazing. My nails have never looked so good and my face feels as if I've shed ten years already."

"Yes, they certainly know their stuff. I hope it didn't cost Sable too much money, it's so generous of her."

"I'm not sure but I think she got it as a favour."

"Really, that's some favour."

"I overheard her telling Finn that they offered it in return for a mention in the magazine she runs."

"Are you kidding?"

I stare at her in shock and she shrugs. "It makes good business sense. A freebie in exchange for a write up. They will get more bookings through it and it's worth it because they would also be included in your wedding portfolio. I'm also guessing their details will be in your hotel brochure; you see, business is well equipped to take a loss leader when it brings great rewards."

"Is that what I am, a loss leader?"

Heidi grins. "Nothing wrong with that if you get to experience this kind of luxury, in fact, I'm thinking of buying a chateau of my own just to see what I can get for free in return for a mention."

I suppose it does make perfect sense and makes me feel a little better. At least it didn't cost her anything, which is a good thing because I'm guessing this place is well above my price range.

We soon head down to dinner and the restaurant is impressive. It's small but intimate and the sight of the candles flickering on the flower infested tables, surrounded by silver cutlery and crystal glasses, makes me wish Finn was here with me. This is a place for romance and as much as I love my best friend, she just isn't who I want to spend the night with. I feel a pang as I suddenly realise that this is the first night Finn and I have spent away from each other since we moved here and I wonder what he's doing.

The waiter interrupts my daydream and I look up in surprise at a familiar face. "Bonsoir mesdames, on se retrouve."

"Beau!" Heidi squeals his name and it feels a little embarrassing to see the obvious delight on her face as she reacquaints herself with the hot masseur from earlier.

He winks and I see her chest heaving from here as she blushes under his heated gaze.

He turns to me and smiles before offering me the menu and then one to Heidi. Her hands shake a little as she takes it and I don't miss the appreciative look he gives her, or the tell-tale blush to her cheeks as she looks down in obvious confusion.

"Puis-je vous apporter quelques boissons."

She looks up and I say rather sharply, "What would you like to drink?"

"Oh, a still water and a glass of white wine please."

She smiles at him and if looks could talk, she would be offering herself on a plate instead of the food.

I order the same and as he leaves, say in a whisper, "What's going on?"

"What do you mean?"

"Him - the flirting, honestly, Heidi what's got into you?"

"Nothing. Can't a girl enjoy a man's attention once in a while?"

"But Harvey, didn't you wake up with him this morning and now you're making eyes at a waiter? This isn't like you."

"How do you know?" She shrugs and I stare at her in surprise. "I do know, this isn't you, Heidi, you've never been the promiscuous type. I'm just worried, that's all."

"Oh, for goodness' sake, Lily, I'm just looking, there's nothing wrong with that."

"Yes, but look where looking got you with Harvey. I'm worried for you."

"Listen, Lily, if I've learned one thing from the last two years, it's this. Opportunities don't come around that often and you owe it to yourself to live a little while you can. Your Aunt's bucket list did sort of rub off on me and travelling with Thomas was exciting and showed me a world outside my own that I much preferred. Now he's jumped ship, I'm left to discover it on my own. You said yourself that Harvey will be gone soon and where will that leave me? No, I need to play loose and not rely on one man to define me because ultimately they could leave at any time."

"But…"

"No buts, Lily. I'm young, free and single and extremely ready to mingle."

She winks and I stare at her as if I'm seeing her for the first time. Who is this woman sitting opposite me? She looks like my best friend, but somehow, she's changed. She looks more self-assured, happier and exudes a confidence I wish I could bottle and sell on eBay and it's as if a powerful force surrounds her. Yes, Heidi is evolving as Sable would say and I'm not sure how I feel about it.

Despite my concerns, we do have a lovely evening and put the world to rights and more besides. The food is heavenly and the place couldn't be more relaxing. Beau is still flirting heavily with Heidi who is lapping up the attention and it only makes me miss Finn even more.

So, as we wait for the coffee, I excuse myself and head outside into the beautiful gardens to call the man himself because I must hear his voice at least.

Tucking myself away in an alcove near a lavender trail, I inhale the heavenly scent and wait for him to answer.

"Hey babe, how's it going?"

As soon as I hear his husky voice, it brings tears to my eyes. "I miss you."

"Well, that goes without saying."

"Idiot. You're meant to tell me you miss me too."

"Well, that goes without saying."

"Honestly, Finn, why are you so difficult all the time?"

He laughs and it brings a smile to my face as I whisper, "Where are you now?"

"Oh, you know, just relaxing with Harvey in the garden."

I'm not sure why, but something in his tone rings the alarm bells and I say quickly, "What's the matter?"
"Nothing."

"Yes there is, I can hear it in your voice."

"No, you can't."

"Yes I can, so, tell me, what are you really doing?"

I hear a rustling noise and strain to make sense of it and it sounds as if Finn is breathing heavily. "What are you doing?"

"Just a little um… exercise."

"But it's 9pm, are you drinking?"

I hear a whisper and say quickly, "Who's that?"

There's a slight pause and Finn says quickly, *"Listen babe, I'm sorry to cut the call short but Harvey needs a hand with something. I'll call you later, love you."*

He cuts the call before I even have a chance to reply and I feel the tears stinging behind my eyes. He's up to something, I know he is.

Quickly, I call my mum because if anyone knows what he's doing it's her and she answers also sounding a little distracted.

"Oh, hi, Lily darling, are you suitably pampered?"

"Never mind all that, what's going on?"

"How did you know? I know, it's that mother-daughter bond that's so strong between us. I've said to your father on numerous occasions, it's like a force, you know, like in Star Wars."

"Mum, what are you talking about, just tell me what's going on?"

There's a slight pause and then she says with resignation.

"I know I shouldn't tell you because you are meant to be resting after all but I'm worried, Lily."

"What about?"

"Mark and that woman."

"Kylie?"

"Yes, her."

"Why, what's she done?"

"She's a strange one, but it's as if she's cast a spell over the castle and is making the men do strange things. They appear to be under her spell and it's worrying me."

"What are you talking about, have you been on the gin again? I thought I told Finn to lock it in the office."

"Oh thanks, I'll go and find it. I wondered where it went. Anyway, Mark is obviously too far gone to notice because he can't see past his own sex drive."

I feel a headache coming on as I say slowly, "Just tell me the facts and spare the rest. What is Kylie doing with the men at the castle?"

I hear her take a deep breath and she says in a whisper.

"She calls it a rare ancient art, but it looks like yoga to me. She has them all sitting on the lawn in very strange poses and is walking among them like a drill sergeant. Only the men are allowed. Apparently, she does a women's class in the

mornings. She told them it was to enhance their sexual power and create stamina and longevity."

Picturing Finn and Harvey enhancing their stamina makes me feel quite faint and I say fearfully, "Is that why Finn was so out of breath?"

"Finn, oh no, he left hours ago."

"Left!"

"Yes, didn't you know, Harvey told us he had arranged a night out for the two of them in the local town? Your father wanted to go, but Harvey was adamant it was just the two of them. To be honest, your father was a little put out at first but then Kylie got her claws into him and he's currently lying on the ground while she straddles him as he attempts a few sit-ups. It's quite disturbing viewing because his face is in line with her um… lady parts as he sits up and I have never seen him so energetic."

Trying hard to banish that image from my mind, I shake myself and say, "What about grandad, surely he's not taking part?"

"Oh yes, darling, they all are. Kylie has a different one for him. This time she sits in front of him with her legs either side and holds his hands as she helps him up and then lowers him back down to

the floor. To the naked eye it looks quite x-rated as
he grinds against her as he comes up each time."

I wish I hadn't called now and mum says sadly,
"It's Mark I feel sorry for. He's been instructed to
sit and watch and not move a muscle. He must
observe and offer feedback at the end of the session.
Does that sound right to you, Lily? This is all a
little weird if you ask me and quite honestly, if
that's what the Australian's do in their spare time,
I'm staying at home."

"What about the others, surely Sable has
something to say about it?"

"Oh yes, Sable has a lot to say but none of it
relating to the extreme sexercise that's going on in
the orchard. No, Sable is ordering her staff around
as well as poor Stella and the nans who are
currently washing dishes and straightening the
place after a very regimented supper. Goodness,
darling, that woman is a machine."

Once again, I wish I hadn't called because it
sounds as if there's organised chaos back home. My
thoughts keep on returning to Finn and I feel on
edge as I picture him on a drunken night out with
Harvey. I've heard what those nights involve and
I'm not happy about it because from what Finn has
told me they make Heidi's antics look tame in
comparison.

Mum suddenly says in an urgent whisper, *"Sorry darling, I've got to go, it looks as if Piers has found me."*

Before I can even ask why that matters, she cuts the call and I stare at my phone in frustration. I have been gone less than 12 hours and the place has descended into crazy chaos and my husband to be is missing presumed up to no good.

I need a drink.

Heidi is now missing. When I return to the table, all that's left are the remnants of our meal and empty wine glasses. Not even a note, just the dying flame of a candle that's on its last legs.

Slumping down in my seat, I reach for the bottle and even that's empty and I sigh with frustration.

Looking around for Beau, it doesn't surprise me that he's also missing and I feel the frustration growing by the second.

There are a few diners left and a woman at the next table takes pity on me and leans over. "If you're looking for your friend, she said she would see you in your room. She needed to answer a call of nature."

She looks at me with interest and I say in surprise, "You're English?"

"Last time I looked."

She smiles and the man with her says politely, "Aaron and Molly Peters. We're from Bath."

I smile and Molly hands me their bottle of wine. "You look as if you need this more than us."

She grins and I laugh self-consciously. "Is it that obvious?"

Gratefully, I splash a little into my glass and raise it in a toast, "To relaxing spa days."

"So, what brings you to Provence…"

"Lily. Well, I live here actually. I part own a chateau nearby and I'm here with my friend on strict instructions to relax because I'm getting married in a few days."

"Congratulations."

They toast me again and Molly says with interest. "That sounds interesting. A chateau seems like the stuff of dreams, what made you leave England?"

"I fell in love."

They share a look and smile and the tears once again build as I think about Finn. To be honest, I'm not enjoying myself half as much as I thought I would because he's not by my side and coupled with the chaos back at home, I'm feeling anxious."

Molly looks concerned. "Is everything ok, Lily, you seem upset about something."

"I'm fine, just being silly I guess, it's just this is the first night we've spent apart since we moved here two years ago and it's strange not having him beside me. Then there's chaos at the chateau, that's where I went, to ring home and it's worrying me."

The couple share a look and Molly says kindly, "Why don't you come with us and we'll fix you a nightcap? I think we've got some brandy in our room and it may make you feel better."

She seems so lovely and it does feel good to meet some normal people for a change, so I nod gratefully. "Thanks, you're very kind."

We head out from the restaurant and I note they walk hand in hand which is lovely to see. "How long have you been married?" They share a look and Molly smiles. "We aren't."

"But you said you were both named Peters, I thought…"

"Coincidence." Aaron laughs. "It's quite a common name and when we found out we couldn't believe our luck. We get to play the married couple without the cost of the wedding."

Molly laughs sweetly. "Yes, none of the expense, no huge wedding to organise and no drain on our resources. Instead, we get to enjoy each other's company with our own little secret keeping us warm at night."

They share a smile and it strikes me that they do seem happy but quite honestly, it's not much of a secret if you ask me."

"Don't you ever wish you had got married though? I mean, surely it's every girl's dream, the white wedding, the romance of the occasion and the fact all your family are in one place to share it with you."

"Not really, to be honest I could think of nothing worse than having my family surrounding me for longer than five minutes."

Molly groans and Aaron nods. "Same, my family bore the pants off me and Molly's are just plain peculiar. No, it's better just the two of us."

They share a look and it strikes me how happy they seem but as I picture my own family, I can't imagine not enjoying spend time with them and feel a little sorry for the nice couple.

We reach their room and like mine, it's luxurious with a simple elegance.

Molly kicks off her shoes and groans. "I hate wearing heels, I only wear them because Aaron finds them sexy."

She giggles and he winks at her before turning to a table by the window and pouring two glasses with brandy before saying, "I'll grab another glass from the bathroom."

Patting the bed, Molly smiles. "Come and sit beside me, Lily, I would love to hear all about your wedding."

"Well, where do I start really?"

Hopping next to her, I relish the comfort of the bed and tuck my legs under me as I proceed to tell Molly my life story. I don't even stop when Aaron returns and hands me a glass of brandy and sits beside her. I'm not sure how long I talk for but find that once I've started, I can't stop. It's like therapy and they seem so interested. It feels nice to be able to offload my problems to strangers as I tell them how my wedding has descended into chaos and the anxiety I feel. Molly nods sympathetically and Aaron says. "It sounds as if you really need this break, Lily."

Molly yawns and I feel bad that I've talked nonstop since I got here and they look tired, so I say apologetically, "I should go and find Heidi. She will be worried about me."

"I doubt it." Molly shakes her head and Aaron laughs. "From the way she was flirting with that waiter, I'm guessing she's otherwise occupied."

My heart sinks. "Yes, she's just broken up with her boyfriend of two years and is fragile and to be honest, it's making her do strange things which is so out of character. Anyway, I should go and leave you in peace."

Shaking her head, Molly reaches out and grabs hold of my arm. "Don't go, Lily, stay for another brandy, it's good having you here and we would enjoy your company."

Aaron nods. "Another nightcap?"

The warmth of the brandy is making me feel happy, so I nod. "Oh, ok, just the one."

He hands me the drink and Molly says pleasantly, "So, tell me, what's your fiancé like?"

At the mention of Finn, I get an even warmer feeling inside and can't stop smiling. "He's everything, you know, Molly, I really think he's my soulmate."

Once again, I talk for ages about everything I love about Finn and they are such good listeners it doesn't make me feel bad for droning on for so long. I think it's sweet the way they share little looks of love when I describe my feelings for him and I love the way he can't seem to stop stroking her arm, or running his fingers through her hair. It restores my faith in love as I really open up to the super nice couple who have been so kind to me.

I'm not even sure of the time when I finally stop for air and say regretfully, "Well, I should go. It was so nice to meet you both."

I make to stand but my legs wobble a little and I fall back on the bed. "Oops, I think I've had too much to drink."

I laugh a little too loudly and Molly giggles. "Oh, Lily, what are we going to do with you?"

She gently pulls me down beside her and starts stroking my hair, whispering, "Let us look after you."

I catch Aaron watching us and something about his expression starts the alarm bells ringing and it strikes me what a vulnerable position I've put myself in. Molly leans down and her face is inches from mine as she says huskily, "Spend the night with us, Lily, let go of your inhibitions and let us show you how amazing that can be."

Quickly, I sit up and stare at them in horror before scooting off the bed and saying nervously, "Um, thanks for the offer but I think I'm going to be sick. I really should get going, it's been great to meet you both but well, you know."

Backing away, I head towards the door and note the disappointment on their faces as Aaron says, "That's a pity, we could have really given you a night to remember."

Molly nods and says huskily, "Please reconsider, Lily, you won't look back."

Feeling the blood rush to my head, I make a dash for the door and wrench it open, saying quickly, "Sorry, I really need to go, thanks for the drink."

I don't think I've ever exited a room so fast in my life and sprint down the hallway towards the stairs at the end, just grateful that our room is at the opposite side of the hotel.

I feel like such a fool. Why did I think it was a good idea to go to a stranger's hotel room? They seemed like such a lovely couple I never gave it a second thought.

It's only when I reach the sanctuary of our room that I feel safe and quickly bolt the door behind me and say loudly, "Heidi, you won't believe what just happened."

However, as I turn around, I can see that our room is empty and it doesn't look as if Heidi has been back at all.

♥*21*

"You're still mad."

We are heading back to the castle in the limo Sable arranged to collect us and Heidi's right, I am super mad.

"You could say that."

"It was really no big deal." Heidi sighs and sinks back in the seat and I say tightly, "2 am. You finally got back at 2 am and could have been murdered for all I know."

"Murdered, you sound like your mum."

"Well, you could and I was feeling very emotional after having been molested by sex pests."

"Tell me about that again, I can't believe it."

Groaning, I fall back against the seat and put my head in my hands. "They seemed so nice. You know, Heidi, it just shows you can never let your guard down even for a second. What on earth possessed me to go to their room will haunt me to my dying day? Please don't tell anyone, my mum will probably die of the shock."

Heidi looks concerned and says in a small voice, "I'm sorry, Lily, I feel responsible."

"Yes, well, if you hadn't gone running off for a night of passion with a stranger, none of that would have happened. What did happen, by the way?"

Heidi giggles and says dreamily, "Oh, Lily, it was so romantic. You know, I still don't understand a word of what he said through the whole experience, but he could have recited war and peace and it couldn't have been sexier. When you went to call home, he appeared and the look in his eyes made mine water. He saw I was alone and nodded towards the exit and I knew he wanted me to follow him. I know I shouldn't but quite honestly that man was every fantasy I've ever had and so I did. I followed him outside and he led me to a spot in the garden that was hidden by a weeping willow. It was so romantic because the stars were out and the sound of a nearby stream gurgling in the darkness made it feel so romantic. Then he pulled me into his arms and kissed me so sweetly I lost my mind. It was probably the most romantic moment of my life and it was as if he really loved me. I know I shouldn't have but I was caught up in the moment and well... you know."

"I'm sorry, Heidi."

"What have you got to be sorry about? I loved every minute of it and if I return home and join a convent, nothing will ever take away the memories of my time in Provence. First my hunky soldier and now my dream French stranger. You know, there is something in this bucket list idea. I always knew your Aunt was clever, but she really saw the potential in this."

"Yes, well, I don't think it was intended as a fuck-it list, Heidi, I think you've interpreted it all wrong."

Heidi giggles and I grin. "Talking of which, please don't tell anyone about my near miss with the swingers from hell. I would be so mortified if anyone found out about my stupid almost ménage à trois. Finn would be so angry and my mum would never sleep again."

Heidi starts to laugh and for some reason I join her. It was certainly an unexpected ending to an otherwise extremely enjoyable trip and so, as we pull up at the Castle of Dreams, it feels good to have gone but even better to be back. For five minutes, anyway.

"Thank goodness your back, Lily."

Mum's anxious face races towards me and my heart twists with fear. "What's happened, is it Finn, surely not nan, oh no, did grandad have too much to drink again and fall in the lake, what about dad?"

"It's *everything*, oh, Lily, I can't cope, nothing has gone right at all. It's the curse of the Castle of Dreams, I just know it is."

Before she can even tell me what's happened, Finn heads towards me looking so normal and so gorgeous, my feet can't help but run at full speed towards him. As he opens his arms, I jump into them and he whispers, "I missed you, Adams."

"Oh, Finn never let me out alone again."

"You're a little dramatic, aren't you?"

He kisses my neck and I shiver. "You think, wait until I tell you what nearly happened to me."

He tenses up and growls, "Tell me now."

"No, later. It's fine, I'm just being a little melodramatic because I really, really, missed you."

As he drops me to the ground, I notice Harvey heading our way and feel the guilt wash over me as I see the smile he gives Heidi. As she heads towards him, my heart sinks because he looks so happy to see her and she appears eager to pick up where they left off. I watch with a sinking feeling as she takes his hand and they head off together without a backward glance.

Mum is still standing there and says impatiently, "Lily, I really need a one on one with you."

Images of the Peters spring to mind and I feel sick as I say faintly, "Ok, help me unpack and tell me what's happened."

However, we don't even get that far before Sable swoops in and says loudly, "Darling, lovely to see you, hopefully feeling refreshed and ready to experience the wedding of your dreams. Now, we must have a catch up, so follow me and I'll fill you in."

Mum sighs with exasperation and I say apologetically, "I should go, she's been so kind and well... I expect she's got wedding stuff to run through."

Leaving mum and Finn behind, I follow Sable to the office and she smiles before closing the door firmly.

"Right then, darling, we have much to do before the preparations start in earnest. In your absence I have organised your family and given them all special jobs. As you know things couldn't continue in the chaotic way they were before you left. Now, you are no longer on duty and are now our guest. Your mum and Stella are in charge of the catering, the nans will set and clear the tables. David and Arthur are responsible for the bar and Piers and Bert are on clearing up duty. Heidi and Stacey are responsible for general housekeeping and Sybil and I will be in charge of the wedding arrangements. Mark and Kylie have been instructed to help with the decorations, so all that is left for you and Finn to do is to relax and make sure you stay worry free and focused on having the most amazing time."

I stare at her in astonishment and she smiles. "I told you to leave it with me. Now, the bridesmaid's dresses are arriving today, so I will expect you all in Heidi's room at 2.30 for a fitting. We need to make sure everything fits and the men will be scheduled in for 4 pm. If any alterations are needed, Sybil is under instructions to deliver them to the local seamstress I have standing by."

Thinking of the horror on Sable's face when she sees my nan's wedding dress, I feel sicker than I did last night and she shakes her head. "Relax, darling, it's all in hand."

I note the fact she is staring at me with a keen look and squirm inside. She has that look in her eye that she always had when she knew I was hiding something and this is no exception, so she leans forward and says firmly, "Tell me what's bothering you."

I laugh self-consciously and then before I know it, offload it all onto her capable shoulders.

163

Suddenly, it all comes rushing out. The anxiety of mum's story about the curse, the worry about Heidi, nan's dress and the fact Mark doesn't seem himself. I also mention about the worry I felt when Finn called and the fact he never rang back weighs heavily on my mind. I even tell her about my encounter last night and she looks angry when I finish.

"I will be having words with that spa, fancy allowing immoral people into their premises preying on unsuspecting victims. I should report them to the police."

"Oh, please don't, I feel embarrassed enough as it is over my own stupidity."

"You know, Lily, it was obvious I was sent here to act as your fairy godmother. You are crumbling under the pressure, which isn't like you. From now on, you are to remain focused and I know just what you need. Come with me."

She marches to the office door and I see mum hovering anxiously nearby, "Oh, Lily, have you finished, it's just that I would really like that word now."

"Stand aside, Sonia, Lily is not to be bothered with any more problems. As the wedding planner and coordinator of things, she is now under strict instructions to relax and regain her inner zen. Any problems you have are to be directed to me, so if you would like to schedule a meeting please ask Sybil to see when I have a window free."

Mum looks completely shocked as we head past and I feel bad but know that there's no stopping Sable when she's in this mood. However, I'm surprised when we head outside to the garden and she leads me over to where Kylie and Mark are working out in the orchard.

Mark looks up as we approach and although he smiles, I see the anxiety in his eyes as Kylie snaps, "Straighten your shoulders, Mark, don't slouch and fetch me my water."

He does as she says and hands her a water bottle and she stares at him pointedly before he blanches and then removes the cap before handing it back to her. She throws back her head and drinks thirstily before handing it back, expecting him to screw the cap back on and place it back on the ground. Then she looks at us and nods. "What can I help you with?"

She looks at me with curiosity and I feel as if she finds me lacking in just about every department because there is a hint of impatience as she studies me, making me feel like something the cat dragged in.

"Ah, Kylie, just the person I need. Lily needs to unwind and de-stress and you are just the person to make it happen."

Turning to me, Sable says shrilly, "Kylie will soon whip you into shape and you start now."

She looks at Mark and says firmly, "Come with me, Mark, I have another job for you."

I don't miss the anxious look he throws Kylie, who just nods. "Go with her, Mark, and remember to meet me back in the room at 12, I expect to see you waiting."

He nods and I stare after him as he scurries away after Sable without a backward glance.

Tuning to me, Kylie says in a no-nonsense voice, "Right then, we will make a start and just so you know, I don't tolerate weakness and am a hard taskmaster. Don't let yourself down, Lily and just remember that I know best and follow everything I say to the letter."

She looks me up and down and I feel as if she is irritated by what she sees because she snaps, "First things first, you need to meet me back here in ten minutes, suitably dressed for a full workout. I will set my watch and for every second you are late; you will be punished. Now go."

I'm not sure why, but I'm off like a formula one racing car from the grid. Punish me, I don't like the sound of that – at all.

I've never been one for fitness. I mean, I love wearing the clothes and everything and grabbing a trendy-looking water bottle and taking some great shots for Instagram, but to actually follow through and do anything never really appealed. I went to a gym once and got some great shots for my newsfeed, but after ten minutes on the running machine, I was bored.

Kylie, on the other hand, appears to have been born in lycra and barks her orders at me like a sergeant major. After five minutes I am a quivering mess and my water bottle is empty. There is absolutely no way I can think of taking any shots for Instagram, or Snapchat for that matter because I can't stop sweating and may not have long to live.

Thinking about my impending passing, I picture the engraving on my tombstone.

'As it turns out, exercise is not good for you.'

"Ok, that's enough warming up, now the hard work really begins."

I stare at Kylie in horror and she shakes her head. "Lily, you are out of shape and this will be the making of you. Now, I want you to run around the lake and I will time you. It should take you ten minutes max and in the spirit of competition, I will run the opposite way and we should meet in the middle."

As Kylie counts down, I am already out of breath at just the thought of running the perimeter of the lake. Visions of me falling into it are at the forefront of my mind and I feel quite ill at the thought of what lurks beneath the surface. Anything could be down there and I absolutely hate getting my hair wet – ever.

Kylie is off like an Olympian, leaving me in her dust. Feeling quite relieved to see her disappear into the distance, I start a gentle jog in the opposite direction. After a few minutes even that is causing me to hyperventilate, so I slow to a power walk instead and think of ways to get out of this impossible situation.

Now I'm alone, I start to breathe again and wonder how my life has descended into chaos so quickly. Before my guests arrived, things were calm and controlled. Positively perfect and now everything is ruined and I blame my mum and her tale of curses and unhappiness.

Heidi has turned into a nymphomaniac in her grief and Mark has returned from down under with a woman who makes Attila The Hun look normal. I wonder about him because he doesn't look happy. It's in his eyes and I can tell he's anxious – all the time. He certainly looks better than when he left and if anything, she has shaped him into an extremely handsome man but there's a sadness surrounding him that I can't quite place. Then there's mum and

dad. Who thought they would be struggling?
They've *never* struggled and all it took to rock their
perfect boat was the fact they were spending more
time together.

I am so lost in thought, I'm startled when I hear,
"Honestly, Lily, is that the best you could do?"

I look up and shake inside as Kylie stands before
me looking as if she's not even out of breath. Then I
notice I've hardly moved, whereas she has broken
the land-speed record.

"Oh, I'm sorry, I think I've pulled a muscle and
thought I should rest a little."

I wince and hold the top of my leg and smile
apologetically. "I'm sorry, Kylie, maybe we should
take a rain check on this. I'm disappointed of course
because I need a good workout but it's not to be."

Placing her hands on her hips, Kylie throws me a
look that could wither a freshly bloomed flower in
sunlight.

"Nonsense, Lily, in order to pull a muscle, you
actually have to own some. You're just like your
brother, weak minded."

I feel my anger bristling as she says flippantly,
"Yes, Mark was just the same when I met him.
Lazy, weak and undisciplined. I made it my mission
to whip him into shape and I'm sure you will agree,
he looks one hundred percent better for it. In fact,
he is fast approaching peak physical perfection and
has me to thank for it. You see, Lily, you only
succeed in life with drive and determination and a
regime that doesn't stop at weekends and on

holidays. Fitness plays a key role in mental health and physical well-being and quite honestly, it's no wonder you look so… well, haggard."

I open my mouth but words fail me as she starts jogging on the spot and says firmly, "Do you want me to save you, Lily? Do you want to look yourself in the eye in the mirror and see a woman who succeeds in life? Do you want me to save you from yourself because if you want to succeed, you need to shape up and make it count? You see, it hasn't escaped my attention that your husband to be is no stranger to perfection. His fitness regime equals, if not supersedes, mine and I'm impressed by his dedication and achievement. Do you think he will be happy to be married to someone who gives up at the first hurdle? Do you think he will be proud to call you his wife when your body gives up on you and you lose your looks? Do you think he will stick around when you can't keep up with him because I've seen it all before? Take his father, for instance. If you have an insight into your own future, look at him. A wandering eye is not good for anyone because it makes his wife feel inadequate and question her own sexuality. It makes him long for something he once had but is now missing because she couldn't be bothered to keep up and that sad story will end in the divorce courts, while she wonders where it all went wrong and he heads off to find someone younger and better than she is."

I've heard enough and say tightly, "If you'll excuse me, Kylie, I think I'm done. It's great to hear your opinions on just about everything you know nothing about, but I would thank you to keep them to yourself. You are a guest in my home and I would ask you to remember that. I'm not my brother and I don't have to take what you obviously dish out to him with every foul word that spills from your lips."

Feeling quite empowered, I stand facing her like a gladiator in the ring and feel my inner Sable rising to do battle, as I say loudly, "And just for the record, the imperfect one around here is you. How dare you judge my family and make out they are failing? You know nothing about us and if I could, I would ask you to leave, so if you don't mind, I will pass on the fitness training because you have absolutely nothing to teach me that I want to learn. God only knows why my brother likes you because quite frankly, I don't, so put that in your water bottle and choke on it."

I turn to leave feeling quite good about myself and empowered by speech. Suddenly, I find myself flat on my back in some kind of stranglehold and appear to have lost the ability to speak because Kylie's hands are wrapped around my neck in some kind of death hold. She sits astride me and leaning in hisses, "You're weak and need to be punished just like I told you would happen. You think your words will be enough to deter me but I have great spirit, Lily and you *will* listen. This is for your own good and you will thank me for it. Now, listen up and listen well because I will only say this once.

You *will* run around this lake and you *will* do it tied to my wrist and God help me if I have to drag you, I *will*. Don't be that weak woman you wear so well, Lily and let the warrior in you out because you may not realise it now but I am giving you the greatest gift a person can receive, purpose and drive. Now, do not struggle because it will only end in your tears because I am stronger than you in every way. Your petulant words roll off me and only fuel my resolve."

She releases me and as I gasp for air, she snaps some sort of plasti-tie around my wrist, effectively securing me to her side and jumps up, almost dragging me behind her. I have no other choice than to try to keep up and every time I try to pull away, the plastic burns as it cuts into my wrist. As I struggle to keep up, it feels as if my lungs are on fire and I can't appear to breathe. My legs are protesting and screaming at me to stop and my chest feels as if ten men are sitting on it and I can't breathe. Kylie appears to be jogging and it's the thought of her increasing her speed that makes me try to keep up because if she accelerated just a little, it's doubtful I would live longer than a few minutes.

Then a miracle happens and some oxygen makes its way into my lungs and as they inflate, it shocks my body into life again. Suddenly, I realise I'm keeping up and a surge of adrenalin makes me feel invincible. Kylie increases her speed a little and I welcome it as I jog beside her. She nods with approval as I match her step for step and soon we are almost running and it feels – exhilarating. Maybe this is what I read about, the adrenalin that athletes can't appear to live without.

As I run, I feel as if I could conquer mountains and swim the Atlantic. Nobody is more powerful than me and I wish to high heaven I had my selfie stick on me because this shot would go viral in a nanosecond were it to make its way to my Instagram feed.

Yes, now I can see what all the fuss is about because I am now one of *them*. The joggers that look as if they are about to crawl through the dusty streets rather than give up and I don't care if I have sweat patches under my arm, or my cheeks are red and prompt onlookers to dial for an ambulance. My body is waking up and there is a brave new world out there and I am the queen of it.

As I run a little faster, my mind inches ahead as I picture myself competing in the London marathon and winning it in record speed. I would hold the record for raising the most money for charity – ever and they would rename it the Lily marathon in my honour.

Yes, I am invincible and Kylie was right, I owe it to myself to graciously accept the mantle of fitness perfection and show Finn just what a powerhouse he is marrying.

I am so busy picturing the Queen shaking my hand as she presents me with my knighthood, I don't notice that we are back where we started until

Kylie breaks my bonds with a flick of her wrist and nods with approval.

"Good effort, Lily, it's a start at least. Now, we will say no more about your outburst and chalk it down to ignorance. Now, head to the showers and report back here at 4 pm where we will continue your training. I'm starting you off at a gentle pace but the real work will soon begin."

She says no more and just turns and sprints back to the castle and I stare after her in amazement. What on earth just happened?

♥*23*

"Room for one more?"

As the water cleanses away my pain, I almost didn't hear Finn come into the room and as the jets calm my bruised body, I wince a little and groan.

"I don't know how you do it, Finn."

"Do what?"

"Maintain a fitness regime that would send most people to an early grave."

He leans against the shower screen and grins. "I see you've had your one on one with Kylie."

"You could say that. What do you make of her because the jury's out with me?"

"She's ok, a little full on but seems nice enough."

"Nice! Are we even speaking about the same woman? I mean, *if* she is a woman, that is. I personally think she's a prototype that's been formed in a lab somewhere as a tyrant perfects his dream race. Surely that woman isn't human, let alone nice."

"You're so melodramatic, you've only been for a jog."

I stare at him in astonishment as he has the cheek to laugh at me. "Jog! If you are referring to my Olympic sprint around the lake, then I can definitely inform you it was no gentle jog. You're lucky that I'm still alive because I'm not lying when I say that for a moment back there it was touch and go whether I would make it to the wedding."

Before I can finish, he steps into the shower and pulls me hard against him and I squeal, "You're still dressed, what are you doing?"

"Shutting you up."

He lowers his lips to mine and I immediately forget what we were talking about as I kiss the man I love, under the jet of water that's washing away my aches and pains. It no longer matters that he is getting soaked to the skin as I help him off with his clothes and relish a brief moment of snatched pleasure in a storm. Finn always has the ability to stop me in full flow and shift my mind to him. He fills my heart, body and soul when he directs his full attention onto me and leaves me struggling for air as he takes over every part of me. The thought of not shaping up and somehow losing this addictive attention, is enough to make me demand every hour of Kylie's time she is here because even though I hate to admit it, her sharp words hit me where it hurt – the part of me that has never thought I was good enough for him. Some would say I have issues and I suppose I do because even in my wildest dreams, I never thought I'd meet, let alone marry, a man like Finn but impossible things happen in life and I'm living proof of that.

As Finn and I get carried away in the moment, I push any doubts away because I know him and our relationship is built on strong foundations. Kylie's wrong if she thinks he will end up like his father because he is nothing like him. Finley Roberts is one of life's successes and the only fault I can find in him is that he is can be irritating to the point of madness – mine and I cannot wait to marry him in just two days' time.

Feeling refreshed, invigorated and so high on endorphins, I head off to grab a sandwich downstairs. As I pass the huge living room that overlooks the garden, I hear my mum calling me. "Lily, quickly, over here."

My heart sinks as I hear the anxiety in her voice because I'm not prepared to shoulder yet another problem, but I fix a smile on my face and head inside the room. "Hey, mum, how are things?"

"Never mind all that, close the door before anyone sees us."

I do as she says but say over my shoulder, "Why, what's the secret?"

"Oh, Lily, I'm so worried."

"What about?" Her anxiety is rubbing off on me and I can feel my euphoria fading. "It's Mark and that woman."

"Kylie."

"Who else? You know, darling, my worry has no beginning and no end with her around. Haven't you noticed how different he is? He may look amazing but quite honestly, he looks well… haunted to me. Something has happened to him and I am going to find out what, if it's the last thing I do. It's my duty as his mother and I owe it to my child to protect him."

She throws me a look that shows she means business and I say in a whisper, "What are you going to do?"

"Well, we need to get them away from each other. Mark needs some distance to shake off the effects of her overbearing personality so he can breathe again. I need you to try and distract her so I can talk to him."

"Me!"

"Yes, you. Maybe do some more of her classes, you know, keep her busy so I can begin the gentle process of extricating him from under her spell."

"Mum, you're not making sense, have you been drinking again?"

"Just a little to settle my nerves because the more I think of it, the more I'm convinced she's got some power over him. You mark my words; I've seen this happen a million times before."

"What?"

"A vulnerable gentle soul in a land far away from home being lured into some kind of weird cult by a manipulative woman."

"Oh, mum, not the cult again, you really should take up knitting or something."

"You may laugh at me, darling but mother knows best. There is something so wicked about that woman and I am not leaving until I get to the bottom of it."

"There you are."

We both look up as the door opens and Piers comes into the room and I notice that mum visibly pales. "Sonia, I've been looking all over for you. I really would like to run that idea I had past you again. Shall we take a walk in the garden to discuss?"

He winks and mum says faintly, "I'm sorry, Piers, but now is not a good time. Maybe later."

"Nonsense, I'm sure whatever it is can wait, this is far more pressing and I will have to insist on your company."

He winks and I stare at him in amazement as he takes mum's hand and gently leads her from the room, saying over his shoulder, "Don't worry, Lily, I'll return her when I've finished with her."

He winks and I don't miss the shock on mum's face as he propels her through the double doors onto the veranda outside. Before I can even comprehend what that all means, Stacey pokes her head around the door and says politely, "Oh good, you're on your own. Can we have a catch up, I really need to run a few things by you for the article?"

I nod and she heads into the room and flops down on the settee and groans. "That feels good."

I feel a little sympathy for Stacey because I recognise myself in her as I ran around completing the task that Sable set me when I was her assistant.

I sit beside her and she says dreamily, "You know, this place is so magical, I can see why you gave everything up to live here."

Looking around, I have to agree with her. "Yes, it's a special place alright."

"And Finn, he's gorgeous, you are so lucky."

"Yes, I am."

Leaning back, she closes her eyes and smiles. "I can only dream of meeting a man like him. How did you meet again?"

I'm not sure why but the way she is gushing over my fiancé is seriously annoying me and I want to shout that *he* is the lucky one, not me. Why does nobody ever say that? It's always Finn this and Finn that and how lucky am I. Maybe it's because of what Kylie said, I'm feeling worthless, so I say tightly, "I'm sorry, Stacey, we really should get back to the article because I'm due to meet Sable shortly to go through the bridesmaid's dresses."

My words have the desired effect and she sits up and pastes her business face back on. "Of course. Now, we need to go through the timeline again and agree what rooms you want featured. I will be poking around a little, I hope you don't mind but I want this to be the best feature the magazine has ever had."

She smiles shyly and I feel like wrestling her to the ground in an instant. Best feature indeed. *I* was the best features editor that magazine ever had and she had better remember that. I'm only here because I fell in love, which means more to me than any job, but seeing her doing what I used to love, makes me doubt my decision. Did I give up on my dream and replace it with another? Is it possible to have both and still win at life?

I feel a headache coming on as so much information crowds to be processed in my mind. Everything is going wrong; I can feel it. Is this the curse of the Castle of Dreams rearing its ugly head after centuries waiting for its moment? Will it disrupt my perfect wedding by seeping into the cracks of a perfect life and pulling it apart before the wedding speeches? Is Finn having doubts, or will he regret this in the future? He gave up so much to be with me and he may already be regretting it now Harvey is back to remind him of everything that was good before he met me.

I shouldn't be feeling like this two days before my wedding, should I? Is it normal to have doubts and where did they come from?

As Stacey drones on about interiors and headlines, my world starts crumbling around my feet. Suddenly, my future is looking different to the one I thought it would be and I'm not so sure anymore - of anything.

♥*24*

"Heidi, you look beautiful."

I stare at her in amazement as she parades around the room in the most beautiful pale pink, satin dress. Her hair is long and curls around her shoulders and her eyes sparkle with the magic that only a designer dress can bring. Sable looks at her with a critical eye and shakes her head. "It's a little tight across the bust and could do with shortening a little."

Heidi spins around and shakes her head. "I like it. It makes my chest heave and look far bigger than it actually is. You are not changing a thing, Sable because I have never felt so good in my life."

Mum wipes away a tear and says with a quiver to her voice, "You look stunning, darling. So beautiful. I can't believe the power of a dress, it's worth more than gold."

As I look at my best friend, I have to agree with her. Yes, Heidi is looking a million dollars, which only makes me dread my own outfit even more.

Luckily, it's still not ready. Nan told me she's having trouble with a stubborn stain and it shocked me to discover I didn't care. In fact, the more I think about the wedding, the more depressed I feel. Maybe it has something to do with the fact I feel out of shape, frazzled and riddled with anxiety. Kylie's words won't leave me and I am comfort eating to cure my depression. The stash of Bakewell tarts and fondant fancies I have in the larder are dwindling fast as I take sanctuary in the comforting walls of a place I should avoid like the plague. I can't believe the woman I have turned into as I battle away my troubles with a curly wurly. When did it all unravel so quickly?

Sybil is next and she looks at herself in the mirror and winces. "I look like Barbie."

Mum rolls her eyes and I stifle a giggle because she's not far off in her description. Her blonde hair is piled high on her head and her dress is so tight it moulds her curves and leaves nothing to the imagination. Her bright pink lips and cornflower blue eyes look good against her pale ivory skin and I feel a pang as I see how amazing she looks. Trying to remember why I thought it would be a good idea to ask such a supermodel to be in my wedding photographs, it all comes back as she turns and smiles at me with tears in her eyes.

"Thank you, darling. I still can't believe you asked me to be your bridesmaid."

"Why wouldn't I? You were such a good friend to me through a very emotional time. I couldn't have got through it if it wasn't for those endless cups of coffees you brought me and the words of wisdom that made everything better."

To be honest, it was never in doubt that I would ask my former assistant. It's true, she was there for me when nobody else was. Heidi was off travelling with Thomas and Sable was here in Provence. Finn was missing in action and I didn't even know if he was coming back. They were dark times and I struggled – a lot. But Sybil was there, rain or shine, a constant in my tumultuous life. Of course, I was going to ask her, there was never any doubt about that.

Mum says in a strangled voice, "I'm so sorry, darling."

"What for?" I look at her in surprise and she brushes another tear away.

"You should be trying on your dream dress with the others. It's just not right that it all went so wrong. There's still time, we have tomorrow, maybe we could travel to Nice and visit a bridal shop there. I would pay any amount of money to make you happy."

My chest tightens as I see the love in my mum's eyes. She's always been there for me, through thick and thin, making my world a better place. All through my life, my mother has held my hand and kissed away the hurt and pain growing up brings. Growing pains are not just physical but mental too and she has suffered more than most as I tossed the arrows of puberty in her direction, wounding her soul with every acid word I spoke. She should have hated me, but she never did. She understood because like most mothers, she was a girl herself once. If I didn't have my mother to see me though those dark days when I thought nothing would ever go right for me and I was destined to a lonely life with no hope of finding a boyfriend, it could have been so different. But she was there, reassuring me that everything would work out in the end and I hope to God she is right because if anything bursts my perfect bubble, I will need her more than I ever did before.

Shrugging, I paper over the cracks and say lightly, "It's fine. It's only a dress and after all, nan married grandad in it, so it's lucky because they are the happiest couple I know."

Mum's eyes mist over and she pulls me in for a hug. "It's ok, darling, you don't have to wear it to make nan feel good about herself. She would understand, this is your day, after all."

Pushing her back gently, I say softly, "Listen, nan's dress will be lovely, the bridesmaid's dresses are lovely and everything is better than I could ever have imagined. The only thing that matters is that I am marrying Finn with everyone I love watching and I would marry him in nothing but a smile if it came to it."

The others giggle at the horrified look on mum's face and then Sable says loudly, "Right then, I'm needed upstairs to supervise the men's suits. Lily, I believe you have another session with Kylie and Sybil and Stacey need to get on with their work. Heidi, you're responsible for rustling up some light refreshments and making sure that the older generation are behaving themselves. Last I saw they were heading into town in the mini bus, so I'm sure they will be back soon with aching feet and more chaos than a person can stand."

As I watch everyone scatter like birds from a scarecrow, my heart sinks as I face another session with my fierce trainer. Two more days and then it will be over. Why is that the only thing getting me through?

25

If I thought my session this morning was hard, this afternoon one was excruciating. Kylie was relentless and had me doing sit-ups, press ups and squats. I had to haul weights above my head and stretch my body into poses that were probably a form of torture during the war. At times I wanted to cry because I am not built for such extremes, but it was only the thought of Finn and not letting him see me as anything but perfect kept me going.

If I wavered it was the memory of the look in Stacey's eyes as she spoke about my future husband. Is this what I can expect, jealous looks from other women, all waiting for our marriage to fail? Maybe it's a good job we are living in the middle of nowhere because I'm not sure my nerves could stand such things on a daily basis.

When did I become this woman who quakes with fear at the thought of losing the only thing that brings me joy in life? Will I become a clinging bore that drives him away after just a few short years?

All of this powers me through the brutal session with a woman who obviously invented the word stamina. She is relentless and unforgiving and I cannot for the life of me think what my brother sees in her.

By the time we are finished, I just want to crawl in the dust towards my room because my legs gave up about twenty minutes ago. As Kylie finally announces the lesson has ended, she jogs off, leaving me on my back, staring up at the sky, struggling to breathe.

The tears that are never far away begin to slide down my face and that is exactly where my father finds me.

"Hey, little girl, what's all this about?"

As he crouches down beside me, I stare up into my dad's concerned eyes and sniff. "I think I over did it, dad."

Lending me a hand, he pulls me into a sitting position and offers me a tissue from his pocket.

"You should be relaxing, honey, not driving yourself to the point of exhaustion."

"Tell that to Kylie. What do you think about her, dad?"

He shrugs and kneels on the ground beside me, looking thoughtful. "I think she's good for Mark. He seems to have grown up a lot since he met her and is turning into a fine young man."

"But mum…"

"I know what your mother thinks, but she's wrong."

"How can you be so sure?"

Maybe it's my imagination, but my father looks down at the ground to disguise the strange look on his face as he stutters, "Trust me, I know. It's not what your mother thinks and Mark has assured me he's happy."

Now I'm intrigued and say with interest, "Tell me, I'm itching to know what it is."

"There's nothing to tell. Mark has found the woman he loves and that's all there is to it. If she isn't the type of woman we thought he'd find, it doesn't make it wrong. People change, Lily and Mark has changed too. It was inevitable really and we must support him in his choices in life."

Now I'm really intrigued but before he can tell me more, I see Finn and Harvey heading my way and know that the fitting must be over already and smile as Finn drops down beside me and laughs. "Good workout?"

He grins at Harvey and I say crossly, "For your information, I could have gone much longer. Kylie had to leave because she couldn't keep up. I was just explaining to dad that I really think I could make a career out of fitness. In fact, I may include it in the castle brochure as an optional extra and charge huge sums for my personal training."

Finn starts to laugh and Harvey says cheekily, "In that case, are you up for a 5 km run? Finn and I were just saying it would be a good way to unwind."

I look at him in horror and Finn laughs while reaching down and lifting me into his arms with ease. "Hold that thought, Harvey, I'm whisking my bride off to the tower for a different kind of workout."

"Finn!"

I stare at him in shock and nod towards my dad who laughs softly, "Don't mind me, I'm off to find your mother. If I'm right, your father will get there first and I should save her."

Finn shakes his head and a pained look passes across his face as he watches my dad head off into the distance and I feel bad for him. It must be hard seeing your dad prowling around like a dog on heat, while your mum struggles to come to terms with how her life has unravelled before her eyes.

Harvey shrugs and grins. "Well, I'm off to see where Heidi's hiding. Catch you later."

He heads off and Finn whispers, "You look exhausted. You need someone to look after you."

As I snuggle into his arms, I don't even care that he carries me inside like a child. I don't think I could walk if I tried and it feels good letting someone else take charge and not ask me questions or put thoughts in my head I never wanted there in the first place. As we take the steps up to our room, I say quietly, "We will be ok, won't we, Finn?"

"Of course, why wouldn't we be?"

"Oh, I don't know, your mum and dad probably thought they would be too but what if the magic dies? What if you wake up and decide you want something better like your father did?"

It surprises me to hear the hard edge to his voice as he growls, "That will never happen, Adams. You are the only thing good in my life and I will die trying to make you happy. If my father can't see the good in his own life, he's a fool. No, you never have to worry about my love for you because I will not be my father, I'll make sure of it."

His words are meant to soothe away my troubles, but they don't. Maybe he's just trying to prove to himself that he's not his father, but sometimes life has a different agenda. How can he be so sure he won't wake up one day and find he's that man he never wanted to be? There are no certainties in life, just fate and I just hope that fate doesn't have some nasty surprises up her sleeve because I never want anything to endanger the happiness I have with this man. Ever!

26

Tonight is supposed to be my hen night and Finn's stag. It's not. Sable decided that there was no way on earth we were partying the night before our wedding and suffering with hangovers the next day.

Instead, she organised a lovely dinner in the orchard that has been dressed for the occasion and is looking so romantic it brings tears to my eyes.

Fairy lights are brightening up the darkness as they twinkle like stars among the leaves of the trees. The grass carpet holds colourful blankets scattering the glade and a huge table covered in a white cloth is groaning under the weight of enough food to feed a small army. Candles flicker in steel lanterns and the soft music of a portable old-fashioned record player is encouraging our guests to brush off their dancing skills. As I look around at our perfect paradise, I wouldn't want to be anywhere else. It's a magical fantasy that is hard to believe and as the sun dips below the horizon and darkness prevails, it strikes me that this time tomorrow I will be a very different person. Lily Rose Adams will cease to exist. In her place will be Lily Rose Roberts and I'm not sure how I feel about that.

As I sway to the romantic music held tenderly in Finn's arms, I suffer a huge identity crisis as it dawns on me that everything is about to change. I'm not prepared to give up my identity with the flourish of a pen and a few words spoken. I won't be *me* anymore and it never really occurred to me until now how that would make me feel. Don't get me wrong, I am so ready to become Finn's wife but a Roberts, I'm not prepared for that.

I spy Piers dancing with Stacey and my heart twists inside me. It's so embarrassing because he is holding her way too close and she is encouraging him. Looking across at mum, I see her throwing death stares to Kylie as Mark fills her glass and then sits at her feet like an adoring puppy. Then I see Stella watching Piers and Stacey with a pained expression.

My heart settles a little as I see grandad Bert spinning nan around the makeshift dancefloor and watch as Harvey says something to Heidi to make her laugh. It all looks so perfect and yet there is an undercurrent that is bubbling along, unseen to the naked eye. This is all a front because this idyllic scene could change in a heartbeat if fate gets her way.

Squeezing my eyes tightly shut, I try to banish any stray thoughts from my mind and just concentrate on the magic of this moment.

As Finn brushes my neck with his lips, I whisper softly, "Um, Finn…"

"Yes, darlin'."

"You know this time tomorrow I will be Lily Rose Roberts, what do you think about that?"

"I love the sound of it."

"Um… yes, me too."

"But?"

"Oh, it's nothing." I giggle to show I'm unconcerned, but he pulls back and frowns. "Tell me what's on your mind because if you don't, I will have to torture it out of you."

"If you must."

I grin and he kisses me lightly and with such love, I almost forget what I was concerned about. Then he pulls back and stares deeply into my eyes. "Well?"

"Oh, it's nothing, really, but we haven't ever spoken about the name thing. I mean, Lily Rose Adams is someone I've kind of got used to, but Lily Rose Roberts is a stranger to me."

"So?"

"Maybe we should merge the two. I don't know, Lily Rose Adams-Roberts sounds so posh and exciting, what do you think?"

Finn sighs and spins me around until we are some way from the guests and he pulls me behind a tree and stares at me with concern. "If that's what you want but why, are you having doubts?"

"No, of course not, it's just..."

He looks a little wounded and I regret saying anything at all and for some reason my eyes fill with tears and I say with a hitch to my voice, "It's all happening so fast. Tomorrow will change everything and I'm not sure if I can keep up with it."

I hate the fact the light in his eyes dims at my words and he says with a voice laced with disappointment, "Are you having second thoughts?"

"No, oh God, no, I want to marry you more than I want anything, even a Stella McCartney dress."

I joke to disguise how nervous I suddenly am because the light hearted ambience of a few moments ago has been tarnished by my own stupid thought process.

Reaching up, I trace the contours of his beautiful face and say with all my heart behind my words, "I love you, Finley Roberts, more than I love myself and if that means I lose a little of my past to gain a future so amazing, it's a small price to pay."

He looks concerned. "I don't want you to have to give up anything for me, Lily. I want you to be happy and certainly not feel as if you're losing something. If you want to keep your name, then do, if you want me to take your name, I will because it doesn't matter what anyone calls me, it's insignificant compared to how much I am looking forward to calling you my wife."

Now I feel even worse than before and a complete and utter bitch and I pull him close and hold him so tightly it hurts my arms. "I love you so much it hurts, Finley Roberts and you're right. What's in a name, anyway? I'm just being silly."

As Finn relaxes against me, I take a deep breath of reality. He's right, nothing matters but us and as we kiss under the light of the moon and the French sky, all I can think of is how lucky I am to marry my soulmate.

We head back to the party and join the others. Betty and Oscar are currently demonstrating Latin-American ballroom dancing, and nan and grandad are struggling to keep up. I laugh as I see how much they are enjoying it as dad films the whole thing on his iPhone. Stella is chatting to mum and Stacey is giggling at something that Piers is whispering in her ear and Finn's face tightens. Squeezing his hand, I lean on his shoulder and notice that Kylie is doing some form of stretching exercise on a nearby tree.

"Mind if we join you?"

Sable sinks down beside us, dragging Arthur with her and looks around happily. "Well, this is very relaxing, isn't it? I can't believe the day is almost here. How are you both feeling?"

She looks at us keenly and Finn smiles. "Like it can't come soon enough for me."

Sable nods in approval and turns to me. "And you, how is the bride bearing up?"

For a moment words fail me because I'm not sure how I'm keeping it all together but one squeeze from Finn's hand rights my world and I smile so hard all my worries escape and float away into the breeze. "I can't wait to become Lily Rose Roberts."

There's an acceptance mixed with determination in my voice and Finn reaches across and grinds my lips to his in a fierce passionate kiss that takes my breath away. We almost forget that Sable and Arthur are here as I demonstrate my acceptance of something that was really no big deal.

We are interrupted by an awkward cough and prise ourselves away and grin at the couple who are struggling to stop laughing.

"Right, I think we should separate you both because you need an early night and must spend time apart, as is the tradition."

Sable looks determined and Arthur shakes his head with a twinkle in his eye.

Feeling the disappointment set in, I look at Finn and say sadly, "Do we have to?"

"Are you seriously disobeying orders, Adams?"

Finn winks and I giggle. "Always."

Shaking his head, Finn turns to his cousin and says, "It will take me a lifetime just to get her to do what I say."

Arthur grins and nods towards his wife. "Trust me, it will never happen."

Sable rolls her eyes and then looks around. "Ok, Finn, we need the best man to whisk you away to the bachelor gîte. Where is he?"

We look up, I can see that he is missing. "Maybe he's helping Heidi with some drinks."

"Yes, we'll head inside and send him out. Now, Lily, say your goodbyes because it's time to send you to bed for the last time as a single lady."

As she pulls me up, I push down the nerves and just embrace the excitement. This is it, say goodbye to Lily Rose Adams because Lily Rose Roberts is a woman who will have it all.

27

We head to the kitchen to grab some champagne and my bridesmaids. The plan is to share a bottle or two in my bedroom and enjoy some light-hearted girly chatter to pass the time.

As we walk into the kitchen, I see Heidi and Mark chatting in the corner, laughing as they eat their way through a Victoria sponge. It makes me smile as I see a little of my brother return and I head over to them and smile. "Any of that cake going spare?"

Heidi nods and cuts me a slice and I look at Mark with interest. "I'm sorry, I haven't had much of a chance to chat to you since you arrived. How are things?"

"Ok, it's good to be here."

"We've missed you; I can't think why, but we did."

I grin and he shakes his head. "Three years is a long time, but it's gone quickly."

"Yes, I'm itching to hear about your time in Oz, what have you been up to?"

"Nothing much, I just bummed around for a bit touring, then I met Kylie and it all changed."

Heidi looks interested as we wait for him to speak and he says a little awkwardly, "She was a friend of a friend and we were sort of thrown together at a party we went to. After that, we just hit it off and the rest, as they say, is history."

I look at him with interest because I want to know everything, how they met, what she does for a job, do they live together... the list is endless?

"So, what does Kylie do for a living?"

"She's a high-powered lawyer. She does really well and you should see her in action."

I share a look with Heidi because I'm sure she *is* good at her job, after all, she definitely has a thick skin and can argue that the sky is green and win.

Heidi says with interest, "How long have you been together?"

Mark shrugs. "A year, 18 months, I can't remember."

"That's a long time, Mark, things are going well then."

He shrugs and looks down and Heidi fixes me with a knowing look. Yes, Mark is unhappy and now I know why - he's had enough.

Playing devil's advocate, I say lightly, "So, what's the plan, I mean, how long are you staying for and are there wedding bells on the horizon for you and Kylie?"

Heidi looks at him keenly as he mumbles, "I don't know. We're due to fly back in two weeks' time. Kylie wants to see Paris and London and we should spend some time with mum and dad."

There's an awkward silence and then I say softly, "I wish you weren't going back. It would be lovely if you could stay here for a while. It just feels like another lifetime since we used to hang out. I'm worried that I won't know you soon."

He makes to speak but Sable interrupts, saying briskly, "Come on girls, it's time to put the bride to bed."

Smiling apologetically, I say softly, "Think about it. Maybe you could extend your trip if you don't have to rush back, Kylie too, of course, although I expect she needs to head back for some court case or another."

He nods and a ghost of a smile passes across his lips as he says matter-of-factly, "Maybe. I'll see."

Kissing him on the cheek, I whisper, "Take care of yourself, it's good to see you."

Sable drags me away before I can say anything else and Heidi says brightly, "I'll just grab the champagne, I won't be long."

As we head upstairs, I can't shake the feeling that something is very wrong with my brother and I hope that he takes me up on my offer, minus his girlfriend because he looks as if he could really use the break.

We pass the lounge and I see most of the other guests have retreated here and are settling in for a night cap themselves. Sable pushes me past the door before they can see us and whispers, "The last thing you need is a conversation with them. You know, Lily, the older generation are more trouble than the young. I've never been surrounded by so many people who appear to have left their morals in the last decade. Do you think when you get to a certain age you just think 'what the hell, it's now or never'

200

because I can't think of any other explanation for the quite frankly shocking behaviour these people pass off as normal."

I start to giggle because she's right. They are all a little peculiar and think nothing of doing whatever they want.

"To be honest, Sable, I hope I'm the same. Why waste your life doing the right thing if the wrong thing is much more fun? As long as it doesn't hurt anyone and is legal, what's the problem?"

Sable fixes me with an incredulous look and says in a shocked voice, "You've changed, Lily. There are rules that we follow in life for a reason, you know. What sort of world would we live in if we did what the hell we wanted to at all times? Anarchy and chaos would rule and there would be no boundaries. No, if you ask me, I think there should be a task force set up to patrol the older generation and issue fines for improper conduct. What good are they to the younger ones looking to them for wisdom and to set an example? Oh no, when I am in their position, I want to spread my knowledge as a lesson to the young on how to live your best life with grace and dignity. I want to be remembered as the woman who made a difference – in a good way and not some party girl who reverted back to her teenage years and ditched her principles in a heartbeat."

I stifle a grin as mum heads towards us, fanning her face with her hand saying wearily, "I don't know how much more of Piers I can take. That man must be on something because he never gives up. Should we rescue Stacey, he's currently got her dancing the Argentine Tango with him and she looks as if she's struggling?"

Sable shakes her head and looks disapproving. "No, let her reap what she sows. That girl needs to learn how to say no, she's always so eager to please, it will only be the ruin of her."

I feel a little alarmed given the circumstances and push any issues I have with her aside. "I think she should come too; you know what Piers is like."

"Oh, very well, I'll go and round her up and see if I can find Sybil while I'm at it."

She heads off and mum says in a low voice, "Shall I ask nan? I know Stella and Betty want to spend some time with Finn but they may be up for a nightcap."

Feeling a little weary, I stare at her with a desperate look and she smiles softly, "It's fine, we'll leave them to it. Maybe it's best we keep this gathering more intimate. You need an early night young lady because tomorrow you won't know what's hit you."

We only make it two steps up the staircase before we see Kylie heading towards us looking irritated. "Have you seen Mark, he was due back fifteen minutes ago, what's taking him so long?"

I'm not sure why but mum says lightly, "I think he was heading towards the lake the last time I saw him."

"Great, just great. You know, that man needs a tracking device, for some reason he's never where he should be these days and I am seriously concerned."

She heads off mumbling to herself and I stare at mum in surprise. "Why did you send her outside? He's in the kitchen, didn't you know?"

"Actually, I did but I'm thinking he needs a little distance from that woman for his own wellbeing, so anything I can do to help, is fine with me."

She moves away looking pleased with herself and as I follow her, I can't help feeling the same. Whatever hold Kylie has over Mark is a strong one, but it's obvious to us that he is pulling further away. Is it wrong to wish they would separate because if it is, I have sinned because the thought of her as my sister-in-law, is not a happy one?

28

Would you like me to tell you a story?

"NO!"

Mum looks surprised and I sigh, leaning my head back against the pillows, feeling just a little high on spirits and company.

"The last story you told us completely ruined the last few days and I am not leaving anything to chance now."

"What on earth are you talking about?" Mum stares at me with total surprise and I snap. "The legend of the Castle of Dreams, remember that? Quite frankly, ever since you told us that story everything started going wrong. Now it's all I can think of. I keep on expecting trouble around every corner and it's tainting what should be a very exciting time for me but all it's done is raise doubts in my mind and cause me bother, so no, no more stories, end of."

Mum looks shocked and there's an awkward silence in the room.

"But it was only a story."

Sable interrupts, looking concerned. "You have doubts?"

I can feel every pair of eyes in the room on me and I shrink back against my pillows, wishing I hadn't said anything. "Not really, but it has raised a few questions. I suppose I was on edge and everything was going wrong and I put it down to the curse of the Castle of Dreams."

Sybil looks up and says briskly, "What did you say the story was called again?"

"The legend of the Castle of Dreams."

She screws up her face and looks thoughtful. "Well, according to my phone and I have put it into every search engine, the only one that comes up is in Bavaria somewhere."

Mum looks a little shamefaced as I stare at her in surprise. "But you said…"

She shrugs. "I *thought* it was this one, I mean, the name's the same. Maybe I didn't check my facts properly."

"Mum, honestly, so what if the name's the same, it was the place that's important? How could you feed me false information on the week of my wedding and then keep on mentioning the curse afterwards, what's wrong with you?"

Everyone looks at my mum and she sighs. "The thing is, darling, I've felt unsettled for weeks. I found the story and yes, it may not have been this actual place but the principles were the same."

"No, they weren't."

"Of course, they were. Every castle has a legend and this is probably no exception, it just probably wasn't recorded."

Mum looks worried and Heidi says softly, "Well, at least it wasn't true after all. You can relax now and those doubts you had can be put down to nerves."

Stacey looks at me with interest. "Well, I wouldn't go through with it if I had doubts."

I stare at her with suspicion as she says lightly, "Well, I wouldn't. Now's the chance to back out before you ruin your life and leave Finn free to meet someone else."

"You would love that, wouldn't you?"

"Excuse me."

My voice raises an octave and I say bitterly, "You've made no secret of the fact you are interested in him, well, bad luck, he's taken and for your information, I can't wait to marry him."

"Is this true?"

Sable looks between us sharply and Stacey stares at me with contempt. "How dare you insinuate that I am after your fiancé? Honestly, Lily, I think you're losing it. I only came here to do my job; which I am sure you will agree is not an easy one. Just because you are unhappy with your own decisions in life, don't take it out on me."

Sable jumps up and points to the door, snarling, "Stacey, please leave. I will have words with you in the morning. Whatever this is between you both stops now. I will not have it, do you hear?"

Stacey looks to the ground shamefaced and I struggle to get my rage under control as I glare at her with daggers. Mum looks bewildered and Heidi says in a calm voice, "I think that would be for the best. We should be having fun, not tearing each other apart."

Stacey sighs and then stands but instead of leaving as asked, comes over and says sadly, "I'm sorry, Lily, I don't know what came over me. You see, to tell you the truth, I am struggling."

She looks down as if she can feel Sable's sharp gaze tearing her to shreds and she sits on the edge of the bed and says sadly, "It's been hard fitting into your shoes. You were always so competent and your ideas way better than any I could dream up. When you left and I was given your job, I used to have panic attacks at night just wondering how I would get through the day. You are a legend at Designer Homes- *on a budget* and a lot to live up to. When I came here and saw this amazing life you had carved out for yourself, I was jealous. Finn is surely every girl's dream and this place – well, it's the fairy tale and I was so jealous I couldn't see beyond my own desire to have the same. If I spoke out of turn, I apologise and for the record, it's taught me a lesson I hope will make me a better person. I fully understand if you want me to leave but I just wanted to say I'm sorry and if it were me, I'd marry that man of yours in a heartbeat because everyone can see yours is a love story that will definitely have a happily ever after."

She turns to leave and reaching out, I pull her back and smile through my tears. "Stay, please. I'm sorry I lost my temper. I've been so on edge I've lost sight of what really matters and if our argument sets me back on the right track, then I should be thanking you."

I pull her in for a hug as Sable says briskly, "Well, thank goodness for that, well said, Stacey but we will still be having that word when we return to London."

I catch Heidi's eye and she gives me the thumbs up and I smile, looking around at the people who have helped me through the past few years and feel so blessed to be spending my last night as Lily Rose Adams with them.

Turning to my mum, I say softly, "Ok mum, about that story, maybe it's just what we need right now."

Looking a little happier, mum sits back in her chair and says in a whisper, "It was a dark and stormy night..."

♥29

Waking up alone in the Castle of Dreams is a strange experience. I have prepared for this day for so long, now it's here it all seems a little surreal. Like it's not happening and is just a dream. It's as if it can't possibly be real because that's what plans are – the future. They don't happen in the present and are a goal that is planned, organised and anticipated – not something that actually happens. But it is. Today I marry Finn and our future is guaranteed. We will walk through life as man and wife and our story begins – today.

It's like a fresh notebook on the first day of school. Exciting, hopeful and as if the last year never happened. It's a day for new beginnings and new promises. The baggage of the past ceases to matter because it's left where it belongs – behind.

Yes, today, Lily Rose Adams gives way to Lily Rose Roberts and I wonder what she's like.

The bed feels empty and cold without Finn to warm the sheets. It feels like an empty void where something important is missing to bring it to life. It feels lonely here in my ivory tower waiting for the conclusion to one story and the beginning of another.

Feeling a strange feeling of anticipation mixed with excitement, I walk over to the window and look out on a glorious day. The sky is blue and the early morning mist has quickly faded, leaving behind a clean sheet waiting for the day to paint a masterpiece. My wedding day – *our* wedding day, it's here at last.

My attention is drawn to the hive of activity in the gardens below. While I slept, it appears that others have not because I can see a mass of people working away below. Flowers are being fixed in place and men and women carry chairs and tables across the lawn towards the lake – the ideal setting for us to pledge our love for one another.

I feel so grateful to Sable because she has organised everything. I have just been consulted and then assured it will be the best day of my life – of that I am certain. I may have had the odd wobble these last few days, but marrying Finn was never in doubt. I want to more than anything and that never changed. He is everything to me and I suppose it was my own inadequacies and fears that made me question why he would want to marry me. Surely there is someone more deserving out there?

A gentle knock at the door distracts my attention and my mum pokes her head around it.

"Hey, did you sleep well?"

She smiles and the sight of her familiar face shining with love, brings a lump to my throat.

"Yes, did you?"

"Not really, darling, a million things were rattling around my brain accompanied by your father's snoring. I forgot to bring those nasal strips he uses and quite honestly I'm surprised you didn't hear it because it was as if we were under attack."

I roll my eyes as she perches on the end of the bed. "This is nice, isn't it?"

"What is?"

"Us, together before the chaos begins. A moment to cherish when a mother lets go of her daughter's hand and hands her to the care of another."

A tear rolls down my mum's face and I swallow hard. "It's not goodbye, mum, it's hello to a new chapter, that's all."

"I know but you're moving on, darling. Soon you'll have a family of your own and won't need me as much."

"Of course, I will, more in fact."

"Maybe, but this is the shift in life a mother never really prepares herself for. The moment when her little girl grows up and leaves home. The moment where I am left at the window waving goodbye, just hoping that I did right by you and taught you how to survive this strange world we live in. No longer there to tuck you in at night and smooth your troubles away, just to be content with the odd phone call once in a while."

"Mum, I've lived here for two years already, nothing will change."

She wipes away a tear and sniffs. "I know, but in my mind, you were always there in that pink bedroom with the My Little Pony duvet. You were still my little girl and now you will be a mother yourself. I'm not going to lie, Lily, I have been preparing for this moment since the day you were born. Such a perfect little bundle of gorgeousness that made my heart complete. I can't explain the feeling a mother gets when she holds her child for the first time and it's hard to let go. But I must because you grew up into a beautiful strong woman and I couldn't be prouder. I just wanted to tell you that, darling, you have become everything I wanted for you and more and if you have a daughter even half as special as you are, you will be the happiest woman alive."

Thankful I have no make-up on, I give way to the emotion that has building for days. Bursting into tears that come from nowhere as it all sinks in. She's right, I'm out on my own and the cosy comfort blanket of home is about to be ripped from under my feet as I am cast adrift in the sea of my own making.

"What's all this?"

Nan enters the room to find me sobbing in my mother's arms and as she joins the circle of trust, she sniffs, "Come on, enough of all that. You're a soppy pair, always have been, always will be."

We smile through our tears and nan smiles. "That's better. Now, I just wanted to say that your nan and grandpa Forest have been sitting downstairs since 7 am. God only knows what time they set off this morning but knowing them it was in the dead of the night."

I look up in surprise as mum jumps to attention. "They're early, I thought I told them to be here at 10."

"Yes, well, time has no meaning when you have so much of it to fill your day." Nan smiles as mum hurries off to find her own mother and father and shakes her head. "I can't think why Dorothy and Ralph didn't come sooner. I know they have an active social life and all, but surely this is more important."

"I think they had to stay behind because grandpa had a golf tournament that he couldn't get out of. It's fine because they are staying on for a bit after the wedding."

"I've never understood golf. Why do men, and some women for that matter, place such importance on knocking a ball into a hole? Madness, if you ask me."

I shrug. "Each to his own, nan. We all have our hobbies and likes and dislikes, it's what makes us human."

"Anyway, treasure, I didn't come to put the world to rights, I wanted to touch base on your dress."

My heart sinks as I see the joy on her face and manage to muster up a small smile from somewhere deep inside and try to look enthusiastic.

"Of course, did you manage to get the stain out?"

"Not exactly, but it's well hidden in the frills. Now, you must follow me because Sable has set up a room solely for you to get ready in. The beauticians are due within the hour and you need to have a good breakfast inside you first. However, I wanted this moment with you, where one bride hands over the reins to another. A girl's wedding dress is one of the most important props of the day and has a lot of meaning. So, come with me, darling, and meet your own dream dress."

My heart sinks as I follow her from the room. At the end of the hallway is a door to a room we have yet to fully refurbish. It's a blank canvas that is waiting for a theme and we ran out of time, so it remains empty and number ten on our 'to do' list.

I can feel the excitement radiating from my nan like a sonic wave as she walks beside me and my heart sinks. This means so much to her and I just don't have the heart to spoil this moment. It will make her so happy and yet a little part of me wishes things had turned out differently.

Stopping outside the door, she beams with excitement. "Now close your eyes little one and trust your old nan."

I do as she says – anything to prolong the moment when I see that infernal dress again and I try to muster up every acting skill I possess so I don't show her just how disappointed I am.

"Are you ready, Lily?"

"Yes." My eyes are squeezed tightly shut and I feel her propel me into the empty room and then say loudly, "Open your eyes, darling."

I am reluctant to do so at first and then as I do, I take a step back and my hand covers my mouth in shock.

What the hell?

Like a mirage in the desert, it stands before the window, the light bathing it in glory. My dress. My actual Givenchy sample sale dress.

I just stare at it in utter amazement as nan laughs softly beside me.

I wander over as if in a trance towards the object of perfection that almost shimmers in the sunlight, the ivory silk gently rippling in the breeze from the open window – *my dress*.

Reaching out, I touch it just to confirm it's actually real and as I feel the silken fabric slip between my fingers; I cry for the second time today. "But how?"

Nan comes up behind me and says softly, "Sable deployed her best weapon and liberated it from the dress shop."

She laughs at my expression. "She tried everything in her power to get them to release the 'hostage' as she called it but they were adamant. It was in the hands of the receivers and was going nowhere."

"So, what changed?" My voice is wobbly and disbelieving, and nan grins. "She sent in the SAS."

I take a step back and stare at her in horror. "She did what?"

"The night you were at the spa, Finn and Harvey were on a mission. They were to liberate the dress and not return empty handed."

"But they'll know it was us when they take stock or something, we could be arrested."

"Unlikely, treasure, you see, they will still have the same number of dresses when they count the stock. The dress wasn't taken, it was swapped."

An icy feeling grips my heart and I stare at her in horror. "Please don't tell me you gave them *your* wedding dress; it means so much to you."

"It doesn't matter."

She shrugs. "They found your dress in a box with your name on it. All they did was replace it with mine, so I'm sure it will return like a boomerang when the receivers complete their paperwork. After all, you had already paid for the dress so legally it's yours. Yes, that dress will make its way back to me and then we'll all be happy."

Staring back at the dress, I try to take it all in. They did this – for me. While I was obsessing over a phone call, Finn was rescuing my dress from incarceration and placing himself in considerable danger for *me*. I am overwhelmed and feel so bad for feeling just the slightest bit annoyed with him when he didn't call me back.

Turning to nan, I pull her into my arms and say with a sob, "I'm sorry, nan."

"What for?"

"For acting like a spoiled child. I know how much it meant to you to see me wearing your dress and that meant the world to me."

"Honestly, Lily, you're such a strange girl. It only meant the world to me if you really wanted it.

Not as a favour to me. How is that a good thing? This is *your* day, not mine. I've had mine and what a fine one it was. They were my choices based on what I wanted at the time. These are yours and you must never let other people interfere with what you really want because this is your life and you must live it how you see fit. You owe it to yourself because ultimately you need to make yourself happy first."

Once again, for the second time today, I sob in a family member's arms. It's too much already. The emotion, the sacrifices and the realisation that I am stepping away from my old life into a new one. However, I know behind me is the fiercest army. The people who will always have my back and steer me on the right course and walking beside me, looking out for me on the way, is the most amazing man I could ever have wished to meet. My husband.

Nan helps me try my dress on and as soon as the soft fabric connects with my body, it's as if all my problems evaporate in an instant. I feel like a princess and as nan fusses around me, checking it fits in the right places and smoothing out the folds, I feel an overwhelming sense of happiness. This is it. My dream wedding is underway and now, with this dress, I can face it head on with happiness in my heart. It's as if the clouds have parted and blue sky and sunshine is all that remains because nothing can get in the way of how happy I feel – nothing.

The Chateau de Rêves has come alive. As we head downstairs for breakfast, I am overwhelmed by how many people are milling around and looking busy. People I have never met before walk past carrying flowers, fabric and boxes. They smile politely but have a professionalism to them that avoids conversation.

Nan guides me to the dining room where most of the guests are sitting enjoying a continental breakfast overlooking the garden. A loud cheer greets me and I smile happily and enjoy the buzz of conversation that brings this place alive. Grabbing a croissant, I help myself to freshly ground coffee and take a seat beside Heidi who grins, her eyes shining. "Morning Mrs Roberts to be."

"Morning bridesmaid number one."

She laughs and spreads a liberal amount of jam onto a piece of toast and says with interest, "How are you feeling today?"

"Amazing. You'll never guess what happened?"

"I already know." She laughs and leans in, whispering, "Harvey told me all about it. It was so romantic. While we were enjoying ourselves at the spa, they were rescuing your dream, there is nothing that demonstrates love more than that."

Thinking back to what we were doing at the spa, mainly her, I frown. "I wish our night had been a little less, um, challenging."

Heidi shrugs and it strikes me that she couldn't care less. "Don't you care that you were being unfaithful to Harvey while he was risking life and limb?"

Heidi stops eating and stares at me in confusion. "What are you talking about?"

"Harvey, of course. The poor guy would be so upset if he knew what you had been up to in his absence."

"But why, we're just friends, you know that?"

"Excuse me if I'm wrong but haven't you spent wild nights of passion with our hero since you got here and disappeared off with him several times during the day? Come on, Heidi, this just isn't like you, what if he actually cares and thinks this is more than you seem to think it is?"

"But…"

Heidi appears lost for words for once and then whispers, "It was only the once. Ok, twice but we had been drinking and the moment sort of carried us away but that's all it is, a bit of fun. You said yourself, Harvey will be heading off soon and anyway, he doesn't think of me like that. Between me and you, I think his attention is elsewhere."

"What?"

I stare at her in astonishment as she nods pointedly across the room and I see Sybil helping herself to a pot of tea looking like a Victoria Secrets model, in cut-off shorts that expose her a little too much and a tight pink t-shirt. Her blonde hair hangs straight down her back and she is oblivious to the admiring glances of just about every other person in the room.

"Sybil!"

Heidi nods, looking very pleased with herself. "Yes, he told me he liked her and I've been helping set them up together. You know the sort of thing, thrusting them together in situations out of their control, forcing them to spend time together and leaving Harvey to reel her in."

"How have I missed this?"

"Well, honey, you have been otherwise preoccupied. You know, I'm quite good at playing cupid. To be honest, they make a great couple, imagine their children. No, I've had so much fun playing matchmaker and it remains to be seen whether they continue this um, relationship, past tomorrow."

Sybil herself wanders over and smiles sweetly, "Oh, Lily, this is going to be amazing. The castle is so romantic and quite honestly I've never been to a place like this in my life. I can't wait to see you marry Finn."

She sits opposite and I stare at her so hard she blushes and looks around her. "What, have I got something on my face?"

"Harvey?"

Heidi giggles as Sybil looks confused and brushes an imaginary Harvey off her face.

"I heard you may be um, getting close."

She blushes a pretty shade of pink to match her top. "Oh, you don't mind, do you?"

She stares at me nervously and I smile happily, "Of course not, it's just…"

She looks worried as I sigh. "It's just he's likely to disappear for months at a time and you will never know when he's back, if at all. I'm not sure it's a good move getting involved with an international man of mystery, I should know, I've been there and ordered the t-shirt in every size and colour."

Sybil nods, looking a little crestfallen, and I immediately regret my words. "I know. I keep on telling myself it's just a moment in time that will end when I pack my bags and leave. It's fine, I'll just enjoy it while it lasts."

Before I can reassure her, we hear, "There you are."

I look up and Sable towers above us, looking formidable in a white fitted shift dress with not a hair out of place.

"The beauticians have arrived and need to work their magic. Its action stations everyone and time is against us."

As we jump to attention, my heart flutters at the thought that in just a few hours' time, it will be over and all of this preparation and planning will have counted for something so amazing.

As I follow Sable from the room, I feel the nerves kick in and wonder if 10 am is just a little too early for a glass of Dutch courage.

♥*31*

"My Instagram likes are lighting up my phone like a Christmas tree."

Heidi looks interested from the seat beside me as the beautician curls her hair. For the last hour we have been taking selfies, group shots and moody shots and posting them on our respective stories and 'sharing' my experience with my legions of fans.

Now my heart is settled and the nerves have been replaced by excitement, I feel like my old self and have been busy capturing the experience for posterity.

Several snapshots of me with my bridesmaids and the mums, not to mention the grandparents, are already eating up any memory my phone may have had left and I am seriously thinking of increasing my cloud storage just to cope. Not that I'm even sure what cloud storage is, it seems like a technical nightmare to me, so I pretend I do and just carry on with my day.

Sable arranged for a bottle of pink champagne to be delivered wrapped in a pink bow and all around me is the excited chatter of women, who are getting ready en masse to look their finest, with the fairy-tale castle as the most romantic backdrop.

However, it seems that every fairy tale has a wicked witch and we soon hear, "Mark, our room, now!"

Heidi looks at me with her eyes wide as we hear footsteps outside and then a door slams so hard it almost makes the castle walls shake.

Heidi looks as if she's about to cry and I stare at her in confusion. "What's going on?"

For some reason she just shrugs and looks away, and yet I can tell she is afraid of something.

I try to put it to the back of my mind but it's impossible and after a while, I excuse myself to use the bathroom and slip from the room in search of answers.

The hallway is empty as I pass through it and I listen for any shouting or arguments. I hear nothing and as I stop outside their room, I wonder whether to disturb them or not. Feeling a little foolish, I turn away and then a loud groan reaches my ears. I stop still as if frozen and listen again. Another groan follows a sound I am unfamiliar with and my heart starts thumping madly inside me as I wonder what on earth is going on in there?

Another noise spurs me into action and I knock on the door loudly, "Um, Mark, sorry to bother you but I think they need you for a rehearsal."

The lies drip from my tongue in a desperate act to disrupt the obvious pain fest inside that room and as Mark has been roped in to ushering duties, it seemed a good distraction.

Two minutes later, the door creaks open an inch and Kylie hisses, "What, now?"

"Yes, I'm sorry but you know, time is against us."

She sounds angry as she snarls, "Fine, he'll be down in five minutes."

The door slams leaving me feeling a mixture of relief and victory because whatever was going on in there, it sounds as if I just saved Mark from some kind of punishment at that vile woman's hands. Vowing to speak to him later, I head back to my pampering a lot happier than I left it.

I never realised just how much fun it would be getting ready with my bridesmaids. We talk, laugh and drink way too much champagne and I am left feeling giddy with it all. As soon as we finish, we all disappear to our respective rooms to get dressed and Sable meets me halfway. "Lily, darling, your hair is amazing, good choice."

Instinctively, my hand reaches to pat the updo that Maryann the hairdresser has so skilfully created. My hair is piled loosely on top of my head, with tendrils escaping at the side. It's pinned in place with diamond clips and a tiara is fixed firmly before it, making me look and feel like a princess. My make-up is natural yet elegant and feels stylish at the same time. She painted my lips the lightest shade of pink and has somehow made them look full as they glisten with a hint of gloss. My nails have been painted to match and I am almost fearful to touch anything in case I scratch them just a little and tarnish what is obviously a work of art.

Sable smiles and I am startled to see her eyes fill with tears as she sniffs, "I feel so proud, my darling.

Look at you, my protegee and business partner looking so angelic and it's all down to my meticulous planning."

As I stare at her in awe, she brushes away a speck of dew glistening in the corner of her eye and sniffs, "I knew it would be the project of my life, and I am glad to see I have risen to the challenge with professionalism and great foresight. I am extremely proud of myself for making this dream of yours a reality and there is no need to thank me, I did it because I love you."

Drawing herself to her full height and seemingly not even requiring me to speak, she says firmly, "It's time, Lily. Time to transform. Come with me."

Transform! Images of those super heroes the Transformers spring immediately to mind and I picture one in a wedding dress wreaking havoc on the guests. Slightly stunned, I follow my mentor to the room where my dress is waiting and try to keep my emotions in check. This is it; it's really happening and now I'm impatient to see Finn and become his wife. All that's left is to 'transform' as Sable put it and head off to marry the man of my dreams in the Castle of Dreams. I can't wait.

This is it. I'm ready.

Savouring the last precious moments of solitude before the door opens and it begins, I look in the mirror and take a deep breath. I stare at the reflection looking back at me and see a princess. I have been totally transformed as Sable expected and the hair, make-up and polished perfection, complements the most exquisite dress I have ever seen. A long lace veil is secured in place and the satin shoes on my feet remind me what wearing heels does for a woman's confidence. I feel amazing and my heart beats just a little faster as I wonder what Finn will think when I walk towards him. I feel quite emotional picturing him standing by the lake waiting for me and I know I will be wrecked as soon as I see him watching me approach.

A gentle knock on the door disturbs me from my thoughts and I swallow hard as my mum and dad head into the room looking the best I have ever seen them. Mum is wearing a pale pink silk dress to match the wedding colours and dad's wearing a black dress suit with a white crisp shirt and pink tie and waistcoat. In his buttonhole is a small spray of flowers made up of one white lily, surrounded by two pink daisies. Mum is holding my bouquet that is a larger version and it brings tears to my eyes as I picture the woman who made this all possible.

Aunt Daisy, the woman I aspired to be, and my dad's sister. The successful woman in the family who had it all except the most important thing – love. The true tragedy of her story was that she had found it only weeks before she had a heart attack and died, leaving us in a state of shock behind her. I found her notebook, in which was a letter to herself where she outlined all her hopes and dreams. She vowed to complete them all, but most remained unticked because she died before the list was completed.

It was only when I vowed to do them in her honour that I met Finn and the rest, as they say, is history. Yes, I achieved what she never did because I have found my soulmate and it's all because of her.

Mum steps forward with teary eyes and whispers, "You look beautiful, darling, I am so proud of you."

She dabs her eyes with a pure white lace hanky and sniffs as dad places his arm around her shoulders and draws her to his side.

"You should be proud, Sonia, because Lily is a credit to you. You have raised her to be an amazing woman."

Mum sniffs as the photographer pokes his head around the door and smiles.

"Ready for the family portrait?"

We nod and as my parents move either side of me, we face the camera for our final moment where it's just the three of us. The next time we pose for the camera I will be a new woman. I will no longer be an Adams and that is still hard to accept.

I take hold of each of their hands and squeeze them tightly as we smile for the camera, ignoring the unwelcome feeling of loss that accompanies destiny.

32

We head downstairs to the lounge where my bridesmaids are waiting and I battle the tears as I see them watching me approach. They look so beautiful and just like I imagined they would. Heidi and Sybil, two important people in my life and I wouldn't have wanted anyone else to walk with me into my future.

Heidi smiles with approval as I say nervously, "So, this is it."

"You look lovely, Lily, how do you feel?"

"Good question, ask me at the end."

Sybil steps forward and brushing a hair from my shoulder, whispers, "If I look half as beautiful as you on my wedding day, I will be extremely happy. That dress was made to enhance your beauty and I am sooo jealous right now."

She grins and a little of my nerves fall away as I realise they have my back. Yes, there is no need to be nervous because this is what I want more than anything and like a dream come true, it's really happening.

Mark appears and I smile happily as I see how handsome he looks in the same suit as my father. For once he looks happy and as his eyes find mine, I see a change in him that makes me question what happened because the shadow has gone from his eyes and he seems different somehow.

I stare at him and he shrugs a little and says firmly, "You are to take your places. They are ready for you."

He heads across to me and leans down, whispering, "You scrub up well, sis, good luck."

Then he kisses me on the cheek and I don't miss the look he gives Heidi as he passes. What the...?

She immediately looks away as I stare at her sharply and my heart sinks. For goodness' sake, even Mark, the woman's out of control. Wondering if that was the reason why Kylie was in a rage, I almost feel sorry for her – almost. My brother and my best friend, surely not, I must have been mistaken.

Mark offers mum his arm and as they walk away, I feel the nerves return. Heidi and Sybil follow them to wait at the entrance to the pink carpet that has been laid on the grass approaching the lake. Either side of it are pink velvet chairs tied with white satin ribbon and decorated with lilies and daisies. The arch itself is white wirework with the same silk and flowers decorating it, set before the shimmering lake in the distance. Everything's perfect and now it's time to make this perfection a reality – *my* reality and now it's here, I can't wait.

Stepping forward, dad takes my hand and says softly, "I really don't want to do this but it's time to give my little girl away."

My vision blurs as I see the emotion in his eyes and I battle my own feelings as I take a tentative step towards my future. He leans down and kisses

229

me softly on the cheek and whispers, "I love you, Lily flower, I always will. No matter what, you will always have that. Now go and get your man."

I can't even look at him as he offers me his arm because the tissues I've stuffed down my bra just won't be enough to stem the tide of emotion heading my way. This is too much, too intense, and I never thought I'd feel so exhausted by my feelings.

As the music changes and starts playing the song we chose together, I close my eyes and steady my breathing, letting the soft sweet music cleanse away my nerves and set me on the right path.

We start to walk forward and Heidi and Sybil fall in behind us. A gentle breeze causes my dress to float around me as if I walk on air. I feel the stares of the congregation as we pass, but I can only focus on one thing. The man waiting so patiently for me to join him and the one I will love to my dying day.

Finn catches my eye and his gaze doesn't leave mine for a second. The intensity of it causes my breath to hitch and my knees to tremble as I see the emotion in his eyes. Finn is not an emotional guy but today has affected him just as much as me because I can see the love reeling me in as I walk towards him slowly, confidently and with a happiness that fills me completely.

My eyes water as he steps forward the moment I reach him, almost as if he can't wait, and we share a smile that closes the world out. Just the two of us matter and we have created a bubble that no one has access to because it's about us – this moment, this day and this ceremony.

He reaches for my hand and as his fingers close around mine, he gives them a gentle squeeze and leans in whispering, "I love you so much, Lily Rose Adams."

He smiles as I whisper, "Right back at you Roberts."

As he pulls me to his side, we look up as Sable stands before us, resplendent in her authority as our wedding officiant. She was adamant she could do it and got her licence in her spare time and nobody was happier than me to have someone I cared for conducting our service. This was exactly what I wanted, an intimate family affair, and it meant so much when she volunteered to help.

She nods and says loudly, "Who gives this woman to this man?"

Dad steps forward and smiles graciously at Finn before winking at me. "I do."

He then takes my hand and places it in Finn's and as his hand wraps around mine, I feel complete.

As the service progresses, I stare only at Finn. I pledge myself to him and mean every word I speak. The vows I say are ones I prepared myself and as we pledge our love to each other, everything falls into place and we are where we both belong. Standing by the lake that has always meant so much to me in the shadow of the castle where we will live and raise our family. The sun is shining and the birds are singing and nothing has ever been as perfect as it is now.

"I now pronounce you man and wife; you may now kiss the bride."

Without waiting a moment more, Finn lifts my face to his and lowers his lips to mine, gently and softly at first, with an increasing pressure that shows the depth of feeling he has. I kiss him back, ignoring the fact several pairs of eyes are on us because nothing else matters than sharing our first kiss as husband and wife. This is what dreams are made of and the way I feel now, is a powerful force of nature because becoming Finn's wife has changed me in a heartbeat. I will not let him down and will be the best wife he could ever wish for because he deserves only the best.

As we pull apart, the page turns in our notebook and I am keen to start writing the story that will shape our lives.

33

Lily Rose Roberts walks down the aisle a changed woman in more ways than just a name. She has found her calling and holding her husband's hand tightly; she feels at peace.

"Are you happy?"

I turn to stare at the man himself and smile with a happiness that can't be contained. "Of course, you?"

"Never been happier."

He grins and once again, leans down to share a kiss and we laugh as Sable says briskly, "No time for sentiment we have a wedding to enjoy. Now, if you stand at the entrance, I will send the guests in one by one."

She claps her hands and Finn shakes his head, "She would make a great drill sergeant, the woman's a machine."

"Goodness, could you imagine Sable in the SAS?"

I am distracted as mum and dad are the first to reach us and there are no more tears. Now is all about celebration and it feels good to welcome Finn into the family and share this moment with the people that mean the most to me. As dad has a few words with Finn, mum leans in and whispers, "You'll never guess what happened?"

"What?" I feel intrigued because there is an excitement in mum's eyes that cannot be contained.

"Move along and grab a glass of champagne."

Sable obviously doesn't realise the seriousness of the conversation we were just about to have and mum sighs. "Find me when you finish, I can't wait to tell you."

She is replaced by Stella who looks amazing in white silk with a beautiful pink and black fascinator in her dark glossy hair. She smiles and pulls me in for a hug, whispering, "Welcome to the family, Lily. You are such a beautiful addition."

There's a sadness to her that makes my heart ache and I wonder if the emotion of the day has got to her too and I squeeze her hand tightly, "I'll look after him, I promise. It won't change a thing though, he's still your little boy."

She smiles with an acceptance that makes me realise she's no different to my own mum. This was also a hard day for her and as she looks over to Finn, her eyes soften and she says, "He always will be but now I have a daughter and what an amazing one she is."

She smiles and moves on and is replaced by her husband, who raises my hand to his lips and kisses it gallantly. "My beautiful daughter-in-law, how did my son get so lucky?"

I roll my eyes and grin because Finn's father is so much like him it should worry me, but it doesn't. Piers is a charmer much like his son, but he's just lost himself a little along the way. He moves along and I watch as he hugs his son and I hope he wakes up and realises what he has is worth fighting for because surely years of memories are worth more than a quick fling with a girl young enough to be his daughter.

Soon we are exhausted with kissing, hugging and welcoming our guests but I wouldn't a change a thing. All the people I love most in the world are here, which is all I want and need. As the final guest moves past, Heidi appears by my side and whispers, "I really need to talk to you."

I can tell it's something serious because she looks worried and my heart starts pounding. However, Sable has other ideas and swoops in, saying loudly, "Take your seat, Heidi, because our happy couple need to take theirs."

Throwing her an apologetic look, I stand beside Finn, hand in hand, as Sable says loudly, "I now present to you, Mr and Mrs Roberts."

As we walk into the large lounge that has been transformed for the occasion, a huge cheer goes up as our guests clap and cheer our arrival. We move past tables decorated with white tablecloths holding similar flower arrangements to the wedding flowers, beside candles in jars and sparkling crystal glasses alongside polished silver cutlery. All around the room are beautiful flowers that scent the room with a heavenly mix of natural perfume and as the guests clap and cheer, I laugh with happiness as all my troubles fade into dust behind me. The relief is overwhelming because now I can just relax and enjoy the rest of my life.

We take our seats which gives me a moment to breathe and I take a look at the scene before me. Our guests are sitting at tables set around the room and the buzz of conversation is the best kind of music to my ears. Dad is sitting beside me and Finn the other and it feels good to be sandwiched between the two most important men in my life.

Finn is deep in conversation with his mother and as my gaze wanders around the room, I smile as I see the two families surrounding us getting on so well.

Leaning across my dad, mum says in a whisper, "Oh, Lily, you should have been there."

"Where?"

Dad shakes his head and throws mum a warning look. "Not now, Sonia."

"She needs to know before she hears it from someone else."

The look on my dad's face tells me it's serious, whatever it is and I say urgently, "Please, just tell me because I won't be able to relax until you do."

Dad holds his hands up and moves back, as mum says, "Mark and Kylie have split up."

"What, how - when?"

I look around in surprise because come to think of it, I haven't seen her at all and feel ashamed that I didn't even miss her.

Mum looks so happy I feel a little bad for Mark but she whispers, "It's quite a story, you know."

"Sonia, please, not now. Lily doesn't want to hear all the gory details, it's her wedding day."

I share a look with my mum because we both know I need to hear those gory details more than life itself at the moment and I say loudly, "Mum, would you help me, I can hear nature calling?"

Dad rolls his eyes and shakes his head as mum sprints forward. "Of course, darling, let me help you."

Finn looks up in surprise as I say apologetically, "Sorry, babe, I may be some time because this dress does not allow a quick visit to the ladies."

He nods and then whispers, "I bet I could get it off in record speed."

Feeling my cheeks grow very warm, I feel a delicious shiver run through me at the passion in his eyes and almost forget I have a juicy bit of gossip waiting, until mum says urgently, "Hurry, darling, things like this won't wait."

We rush up the stairs to her room as quickly as heels and the longest dress in the world will allow, passing the waiters heading past with the starters and mum says apologetically, "Maybe this should wait, I don't want to ruin your wedding feast."

With a determination that shows me what's more important to me, I hiss, "Oh no, I need to know now, otherwise I will definitely *not* enjoy my wedding feast as you put it."

By the time we reach her room, I'm a mass of nerves. It must be something serious given the looks on their faces and I remember the one on Heidi's mirrored theirs, so I look at mum anxiously as she closes the door.

"Well?"

"Where do I start?"

"Maybe cut the reason why and fill in the gaps later. We only have a minute, after all."

"Ok, well, here goes. It turns out that I was right, Kylie did have Mark entrapped in a weird situation and he was brainwashed."

"The cult?" I say the word with fear in my voice because I can't believe she was right all along.

However, mum shakes her head. "Something like that, he was her sex slave."

34

"Are you ok, darlin'?"

Somehow, I make my way back to my seat as if on autopilot. I actually can't believe what my mum just told me and can't look in Mark's general direction.

Nodding, I take my seat and reach for the champagne and to Finn's surprise, down it in one.

He leans across looking concerned. "What is it?"

My eyes are wide and I whisper, "It's Mark."

"Is he ok?"

Finn looks worried and his eyes go in search of my brother who is laughing happily at something Harvey is saying to him just a few seats along. "He seems ok to me."

"Well, looks can be deceiving. He's split up from Kylie just before the wedding."

Finn looks down and I can tell he is trying not to laugh. "I see."

"What do you see, Finn because I doubt in a month of Sundays you will have seen this one coming? I'm not going to lie; I am shocked beyond belief quite frankly and on my wedding day too."

Finn starts to laugh and then it strikes me that he doesn't seem surprised at all and I say incredulously, "You knew?"

Leaning across, he whispers, "I had my suspicions."

He turns as mum taps him on the shoulder and I sink back in my seat wearily. Finn knew. If Finn knew, Harvey knew, and probably everyone else in this castle except me, my mum and…"

As I look around, it occurs to me that we were probably the only people who didn't know and once again, I take another gulp of the champagne that the waiter has just refilled and look across at Mark in a new light. No wonder he looked so unhappy; I can't believe he would allow himself to be used in that way. Then I watch as he looks the length of the table and finds Heidi and the look that passes between them shows me there is way more to this story than mum just told me. Mark and Heidi, how do I feel about that?

I pick at my starter, obsessing over the information I just heard and am only distracted when a flash of pink catches my attention and I see Sybil disappear through the side door. Then I watch Harvey follow her and it strikes me that while I've been obsessing over my own nerves and feelings, things have been playing out around me without me even realising. Leaning towards Finn, I whisper, "Did you know about Harvey and Sybil?"

"Yes."

"And you never told me."

"Didn't get the chance."

He grins and I say crossly, "You knew I'd want to know, after all, I did think he was having a fling with Heidi."

"They were, but it was just that, a fling. When Sybil arrived, his attention shifted onto her."

"That's disgusting."

"That's Harvey."

He laughs and then raises his glass to mine and whispers, "To us and a long and happy life together."

As we clink glasses, nothing else matters. So, what if all the guests are swapping rooms and partners, all that matters is that we don't? Yes, I will stay loyal to this man because I will never meet anyone who completes me like he does.

It takes us exactly one hour to eat the food that probably took the caterers months in planning and days to create. It was worth every email back and forth as Sable struck the usual deal with them for a huge discount in exchange for free advertising in our wedding brochure.

As soon as the last plate is cleared away, it's time for the speeches and we look at Harvey with expectation as he beams around the room before calling on my father to say a few words.

He stands and I fight back the tears before he even speaks as he looks at me softly and says in a loud voice, "Today is not only Lily's dream but mine too. From the moment I saw her for the first time, I knew she was special. My little girl. She will always be my little girl because that doesn't change with a signature on a piece of paper or a change of surname. The only thing that *has* changed is that I am trusting someone else to look out for her.

Someone who will care for her and treasure her as she deserves. You see, the man who has captured her heart is the luckiest man alive because I know he will enjoy a life filled with love and companionship and the loyalty of a woman who will be strong, loyal and faithful and make his life amazing. I should know because I married such a woman myself and it is down to her that our two children have turned out to be so magnificent. So, before I raise a toast to my daughter and new son-in-law, please raise your glasses to the woman of my dreams, Sonia."

We all raise our glasses and the look on mum's face speaks more than a thousand words, as dad leans down and kisses her so sweetly it brings tears to my eyes.

Then dad stands and turns to Finn, saying warmly, "Welcome to the family, Finn, I really mean that because if I could have chosen a husband for my daughter, it would have always been you. I am trusting you with my most precious thing in life and more than anything, I hope you don't let me down because if you do, it will take a brave man to teach you the error of your ways."

We all laugh as dad turns to me and his eyes soften as he says, "And to you, Lily Rose, may you be as happy as your mother has made me because then I know you'll be fine. Always remember you have the love of a good family behind you, both in your own and your new one and we are so happy that you found such a good one to share your life with. So, please raise a toast to families everywhere and especially to the two people who are just starting theirs."

"To families."

We all raise our glasses as dad hands over to Finn, who stands and smiles gratefully.

"Thank you, David, I just want you to know that you have nothing to worry about. When I met Lily, it was touch and go there for a while. She was annoying, argumentative, headstrong and challenging, and I should have walked away immediately. But where was the challenge in that and as you all know; I love a challenge?"

We laugh as he reaches down and takes my hand and pulls me up to stand beside him.

"You all know that the reason we met was because of Lily's quest to complete her Aunt Daisy's bucket list. Thank goodness we did because it made me look at my own life a little differently and question my choices. Lily's choices, on the other hand, were a little strange. I mean, who takes a wheelie case on a camping expedition filled with facemasks and sleep spray? I should have known then she was trouble. But the night she visited me in my tent and begged to sleep with me, I began to see her in a different light."

I stare around in horror and say loudly, "It wasn't like that, tell them, Finn."

Finn shrugs as the guests laugh, "I state the facts, Adams and you change them. Well, as soon as I pulled that strange fleece-covered body into my arms, I knew immediately I was never letting her go. I had been searching for her all my life and although I told her we needed to snuggle up to survive the extreme temperatures outside, I knew it was for a different reason. Lily was my future and the person who made my world spin and my heart beat a little faster. She was everything and so I made it my new mission to win her heart. Now we are husband and wife and like all special force's operatives, 'he who dares wins.' Well, I won big time, so raise your glasses to my beautiful bride and the only woman who has ever made me question my own sanity on a daily basis. Life is certainly interesting with her around, so to you, Lily, I will love you forever and promise me you'll never change."

Finn kisses me as everyone calls our name in a toast and I melt into him as if we are one person. As we pull back, I stare into those compelling eyes and say in a loud voice, "My turn."

Finn rolls his eyes, "Of course you want to say something,"

"Well, you don't get to say things and not let me speak. That's not how it works these days."

"You just have to have the last word, don't you, Adams?"

"Of course, it goes without saying."

He laughs softly and I turn to face the guests.

"When I met Finn, I thought he was arrogant, conceited and definitely not my type. The only thing he had was seriously good looks, but his ego overshadowed that. However, the idiot crawled inside my heart from the moment he shared his body with me – sorry, I meant warmth from his body."

Finn grins and winks as the laughter rolls around the room like a Mexican wave.

"Well, when the trip ended, I was upset because it meant I never got to see him again. However, he had other ideas and what followed next was so romantic, I still can't believe it to this very day. The results of which are here all around you. Somehow, we ended up here in the Castle of Dreams and it's been hard and difficult at times but we have made it. This place is the result of all our hard work and we couldn't have done it without our friends Sable and Arthur. So, to friends, pulling together and following your dreams because where they take you is worth the effort involved. To my new husband who has to put up with a lot but does so with good humour and a love that I will never take for granted. To friends and family and stepping outside your comfort zone because that is where the real riches lie. Last of all, I want to say in front of everyone, I love you, Finn, to the moon and back and I always will."

Once again, as the toasts fill the room, I pull my husband towards me and kiss him with my whole heart behind it.

Then, as we pull apart, a loud voice says, "It's my turn now."

Groaning, we take our seats as Harvey stands with a wicked grin and taps his glass with his spoon.

"For those who don't know me, I am Finn's best man. Emphasis on the word 'best.' Yes, I always was the best at everything. The best soldier, the best fighter, the best lover and the best at just about every task we were set. However, Finn has beaten me for once in his life because he has found the secret we are all searching for and has given everything up to make it happen. Finn found love and the only woman on earth who would actually put up with him for five minutes, let alone a lifetime. Lily *is* that woman and he couldn't have chosen better. She is everything he always said he wanted when we were lying under the stars in a war-torn country, hungry, starving and smelling like dogs. Yes, it's hard to believe he gave all that up for love – what's the matter with you, bro?"

We laugh as Harvey turns his attention to the bridesmaids.

"Lily has some amazing friends who have risen to the challenge of being her bridesmaids. I can definitely say I approve of her choices because I have made it my mission to…"

"Harvey!"

Mum nudges him and he grins wickedly as Heidi squirms just a little in her seat.

His eyes fall on Sybil and I see a slight hesitation in the normally cocky young soldier, as he says softly, "Seeing Finn so happy may have rubbed a little off on me because I have recognised the importance of love and finding someone who makes you question every choice you made in life. Finn and Lily have taught me the importance of partnership and being in a different kind of team and so I thank them both for ruining my life because now I have a decision to make of my own."

I think my heart stops beating as I look at Sybil and note the tears in her eyes as she stares at him with an expression that I recognise – love. Harvey appears to shake himself and says brightly, "Anyway, Finley has been in my team for many years now and the stories I could tell would make your hair curl."

"Please don't."

Finn throws him a warning look and Harvey holds his hands up. "Find me later ladies and gentleman and I'll tell you everything because you will not believe what that man is capable of."

He raises his glass and says loudly, "To the happy couple and the two bridesmaids who were, quite simply, my reason for agreeing to this gig in the first place."

As we raise our glasses, I breathe a sigh of relief. Well, that could have been a whole lot worse.

♥35

Once we've cut the cake, Sable ushers us into the television room where she has arranged extra seating in front of the huge television that was Finn's pride and joy when we set this room up. I look at her in surprise because I haven't got a clue what she is about to show us.

As the last person takes their seat, she stands at the front and smiles happily.

"As you all know, this Castle has been a dream of Arthur's and mine for some years now and we were so happy when Finn and Lily agreed to share it with us. Well, I can reveal to you today the progress we have made and introduce you to the premier of our promotion video that we will use to drum up interest for happy couples everywhere to spend some quality time here in provincial paradise. I must say, it was touch and go whether it would be ready on time, but I received the final recording this morning. It was delayed a little because I wanted it as up to date as possible and we were just retrieving the information from the drone I arranged to record the final pictures."

"Did you know about this?" I whisper to Finn and he shakes his head. "No, nothing."

Arthur stands beside his wife and looks excited. "It was a surprise for the happy couple as a reward for all their hard work and we dedicate this video to the two of you, who without all your hard work, none of this would be anywhere near as impressive as it is now. So, without further ado, I give you the Castle of Dreams."

As he presses play, I am riveted to the screen. As videos goes, it's impressive. Images of the castle in its unrestored state, flood the screen and brings tears to my eyes as we see a snapshot of our past when it all began. Finn squeezes my hand tightly as we share this moment because it brings it all back. The crumbling walls and weed strewn paths. The noise and hustle and bustle of the builders who called this place home for two long years. As it goes on, we see the castle transformed from a ruin to a palace and the tears burn my eyes with pride and love for such a jewel in Provence. As the landscape changes with the seasons, we see the gardens burst to life once again and the past replaced with the present, as the lawns are now cut and resemble a bowling green. The orchards groan under the weight of the fruit where once the weeds had free rein. The battered paths are brought back to glory and the flower beds dug over and planted with flowers and shrubs that make people gasp. Raised vegetable beds, sit proudly in a walled garden with their well-tended rows bearing the fruits of hard labour to feed the occupants inside. The castle shines like a jewel in the sunlight as it's brought to life again and the tears run freely down my face as all the hard work of the last two years reaches a climax on this, our special day. Then it all changes and my tears fall for a different reason as Betty calls out, "Good god, is that you, Lily?"

My heart stops as my face fills the screen in glorious technicolour as I grind against Finn by the side of the lake, leaving absolutely nothing to the imagination. Sable cries out, "Arthur, stop it immediately."

As Arthur struggles to find the remote, the damage is done as every single one of our guests watch Finn and I making passionate love by the side of the lake with the Castle of Dreams reflected in the background. I stare in horror as I share my most intimate moment with my entire family and the shocked silence highlights the fact that absolutely everyone has seen it.

My dad jumps up and stands in front of the television trying to get his jacket to cover the outrageously large screen and then Finn starts laughing fit to burst as Harvey joins in. I catch my mum's eye and she has tears of laughter rolling down her face as nan says, "Bit of a chip off the old block, isn't she Bert. Do you remember that time...?"

"Mother!"

Dad looks furious as Betty laughs. "Good god, that's the highlight of my day, people pay good money to see this type of thing."

Finn looks at me and laughs even harder as I stare at him in compete mortification as Stella says primly, "Honestly, Finn, nothing ever changes, you just lie back and let Lily do all the work."

Now the tears are falling for a different reason and I can't breathe for laughing. Heidi is clutching her sides and the look she gives me tells me I'm not one to judge. Piers and Stella laugh fit to burst and Nanny Forest looks around the room in amazement as she says, "What's so funny?"

Grandad Forest's laugh can be heard in Paris as he booms, "Don't act the innocent, Dorothy, it's nothing we haven't done countless times before."

I think it takes us a good thirty minutes before we settle down and Sable says apologetically, "Um, well, obviously there will be some tweaks before we can make it public and as wedding videos go, it does go a step too far but anyway, moving on."

She claps her hands and says loudly, "The photographer is set up in the garden and we should all make our way outside to pose for the camera."

"Don't worry, Lily's a natural." Harvey shouts, sending us all into fits again and Sable shakes her head wearily. "I need a drink. Arthur fetch me a bottle of prosecco with a straw, I'll be the one collapsed in a heap in the garden."

They head off and mum shakes her head. "Whatever next. I blame you for this, David."

"Me? Why is this my fault?"

"They take after you, both of them. Sex on the brain, morning, noon and night."

She squeals as my dad chases after her and Finn laughs, before whispering, "Are you ok, babe, sorry about that."

"It's fine. A little embarrassing, I'll admit, but who cares anyway, just make sure it's edited out before anyone else sees it, I'm begging you."

Laughing, he sweeps me into his arms and kisses me long and hard, before saying, "Come on, let's go and take some photos we can share with the world and save the x-rated version for our wedding night."

"I'm exhausted."

I shrug off my shoes that have been crippling me for most of the day and let the grass tickle my toes. After the endless photographs, we partied hard in the garden where there were comfy chairs, cushions and little tables to rest our drinks as we danced to the sound of the local band that Sable, of course, arranged.

I have danced with every person here and chatted endlessly with the various groups but now it's just me and Heidi and a bottle of wine and an extremely long overdue conversation.

"So, confess everything, what really happened with Mark and Kylie?"

Heidi sighs and even in the darkness, I see a shadow cross her face as she says sadly, "When I first saw Mark again, it was the sadness inside him that struck me first. I watched him a lot and I don't know; something struck a chord with me and I found myself looking for him in a crowded room. I kept on telling myself he had a girlfriend and I was fooling around with Harvey, anyway. Then it all changed when we found ourselves alone in the kitchen one day. We got talking and he seemed to relax before my eyes. I found out we had so many things in common and soon we started seeking each other out when the coast was clear. Kylie was busy with her fitness classes and Mark and I took full advantage of that. Not in the way you think, but to talk."

"Talk, are you kidding me?"

"No really, just talk. He opened up to me and told me how unhappy he was. Apparently, when Kylie first met him, he was a mess. He told me he had dabbled in things he shouldn't and consequently had no money or job. He was failing and didn't know what to do about it, so she took him in, in return for one thing."

I almost don't want to hear it but she whispers, "Sex. If she cared for him, gave him a place to stay, food to eat and a place to call home, he had to give himself to her in every way."

Heidi shakes her head, saying sadly, "He told me he thought it was fun at first and couldn't believe his luck. She was older than him and taught him things he never dreamed of."

"I bet she did."

I feel angry that he was used in this way, but Heidi shrugs. "He loved it at first, but then things took a dark turn."

"What do you mean?"

"Oh, Lily, you've read Fifty Shades, she was the equivalent of Christian Grey. She used to tie him up if he did anything wrong and well, you know…."

"What?" I can't imagine Mark doing anything that would require imprisonment but Heidi says with a hint of disbelief in her voice, "Apparently, she was fond of the whip and used to whip him within an inch of his life if he forgot to put the bins out."

I feel sick and she shrugs. "After a while, he was so far gone he couldn't walk in the wrong way and she would punish him. He told me that it all came to a head when they came here. Suddenly, he was ashamed of his life and ashamed of her. Being surrounded by his family again made him realise what he was missing and he wanted out. When we heard them arguing, he told her he wasn't going back with her. Apparently, she flew into a rage and tried to handcuff him to the bed and beat him into submission. Then you knocked on the door and interrupted her moment of madness. He took his chance and told her to get out, or he would tell everyone what she did. Knowing he had absolutely everyone on his side, she packed her bags and left."

"Where did she go?"

"I think she got a cab into town to stay at the local hotel. Mark told me he expects she will fly home as soon as she can change the tickets because she won't want to stay here without him."

"But what happens now, I mean, where do you fit into all this?"

The smile on Heidi's face tells me everything I need to know because she says softly, "If it's ok with you, we are both going to stay here and help out. I hope that's ok because we would really like to see where this thing goes. I mean, since Thomas left me, I've been a little crazy myself."

"You don't say?"

I smile to take the sting from my words and she reaches across and squeezes my hand. "I'm so excited for the future for the first time in ages and it's all because of him. They say you know when you meet the love of your life and it's true, I really think it is. Mark and I have only shared a kiss or a hundred and yet that's enough to know we want to do this thing right, carefully, and let our love develop slowly so it stands the test of time. It would be easy to take it further, but both of us are not in any hurry to rush something that could be so special. We bear the scars of what happens when you do and I know you find this so hard to believe but I'm a changed woman since I met him."

Hearing Heidi speak and sitting beside my best friend on the happiest day of my life, who am I to question what she feels? If anyone knows about destiny, it's me, so I reach across and hug her warmly, saying with a great deal of emotion, "I'm happy for you, babe and of course you can stay, we need you more than you realise."

"Here you are."

We look up as Mark sits on the floor at our feet and appears a little anxious. "Is everything ok, did Heidi tell you?"

Nodding, I smile. "I'm happy for you, Mark. I can't believe you went through so much, but that's in the past now. I'm just glad you're home now with people who care and love you. Anyway, I'm a fine one to talk. At least you haven't made a sex tape and premiered it in front of your whole family, including your new mother-in-law. I doubt I will ever live this one down."

He smiles and it's as if everything settles into place where it should be. Mark and Heidi, I certainly never saw that coming.

♥*37*

The band plays my favourite song and I am in the arms of my favourite person in the world and life doesn't get any better than this. As Finn and I dance slowly in a little clearing, surrounded by family, I am lost in a little piece of heaven. I can feel the steady thump of his heart as I press my cheek against his chest and his arms hold me firmly and yet as if I'm a precious glass object that could break at any time.

The sun has long left us and the moon is shining brightly as it watches over the earth as it sleeps. But there is no time for sleeping yet because this a day that should last forever because it's the one I've been waiting for all my life.

As I steal a glance at the world outside my protective bubble, I see my parents swaying a short distance away and I smile to myself. They look so happy as they dance in the moonlight with my mum's cheek pressed to dad's chest in much the same way as mine is now. They have always been happy which gives me faith for my own future because I feel a sharp pain as I see Stella wrapped in a blanket staring at the ground as she huddles in a seat on the edge of the dance floor. Piers is dancing with Stacey who should know better a short distance away and I feel so bad for Stella who deserves so much more. Sighing, I lean back and whisper, "I think you should dance with your mum; she looks a little lonely over there."

Following my eye, Finn nods. "I could kill my dad, what's he playing at?"

"I'm not sure but whatever it is, there's nothing we can do but be there for her. I'm sure they'll work it out eventually, but it's hard to be happy when someone you care about obviously isn't."

Finn nods and then presses a kiss to my forehead and sighs, "I'll be right back, let me check on her and then we can leave them all to it, it is our wedding night, after all."

A delicious shiver of expectation reminds me that the best is yet to come and as I watch my husband approach his mother, I love the way her face lights up the minute she hears him call her name. I know that feeling because every time I see him my heart beats just that little faster and I congratulate myself on finding a man who is perfect for me in every way.

For a minute, I watch my guests as they settle down after an eventful day. Mark and Heidi are wrapped in each other's arms as they dance alone in a crowd. They appear to only have eyes for each other and I am looking forward to watching their love blossom over the coming months. Will it work? Who knows but I hope it does more than anything because they are the two people closest to me and it's the selfish part of me that wants it probably more than they do.

Then I see Harvey and Sybil dancing so closely I'm not sure where he ends and she begins. Will they follow in our footsteps? I hope so because if they find half the love I have for Finn, I know they will be happy. Sybil has never found a man who can keep her attention for long and from what Finn has told me, Harvey is the biggest rogue there is, which is why I think they'll be just fine.

My grandparents are sitting with Finn's and I smile at the happiness in their little circle as the laughter rises above the music, reminding me that love can indeed stand the test of time. All of them have stayed together and shared lives that haven't always been easy, but they have pulled through with love and good humour. Will that be us in the future, watching our grandchildren set off on their own path with the one they love? I certainly like to think so. I just hope that we are so lucky and like them, have a lifetime of memories to think back on with no regrets.

"Penny for them, darling."

I smile as Sable stands beside me on the edge of the group.

"I was just thinking about love and life. You know, Sable, my life has changed so much in such a short space of time, I'm just catching up with it. The day you told me you were leaving and coming to live here changed everything for me. At the time I thought you were mad because I couldn't imagine you anywhere but behind your desk in the city you were born to rule. I never for one minute thought my own life was about to change direction and it would actually be me who was set to take a different path. It's funny how life works out, isn't it?"

"It certainly is. You know, Lily, when Arthur and I first saw The Castle of Dreams it was anything but. As you know, it was a crumbling ruin that stared out at us from a computer screen and we saw a project, nothing more. It was a business idea to make us even more money and provide us with something to sink our teeth into. We never looked behind that opportunity to see what a special place this really is. When I left London and came here to project manage our idea, that was all it was. I never fell in love with the place itself, just saw all the problems it presented to me on a daily basis. It became an albatross around my neck and I began to hate the very sight of it. You, on the other hand, always saw it differently. You looked behind the façade and saw the place it always was. The heart of a fantasy and a place that would reflect your own hopes and dreams. You fell in love twice that winter, once with Finn and the second time with this place and that is why it is you who will make this a success, where I was doomed to fail. This was never my dream, not really. I never connected with its soul like you and Finn did, which is why I am so happy for you both because you have found the place you both belong and the castle has found its King and Queen. But you don't have to do it alone, darling, because you are surrounded by many

261

willing pairs of hands. So, shake off the responsibility and enjoy the fairy tale and I hope you will live happily ever after because if anyone deserves to, it's you."

To my surprise, Sable slips her arm around my shoulders and for a moment we stand and look up at the Castle of Dreams that looks over the wedding it never got to see. Was mum's story just a figment of somebody's imagination, or was it real? We will never know the answer to that but I like to think that whatever curse may have been put upon this place in the past, is now replaced with a different kind of magic.

Sable interrupts my daydream and says briskly, "Anyway, there is one more surprise for the happy couple before bed, which is why I need you and Finn to follow me."

I turn and look at her in surprise as she nods to Arthur who leans down and whispers to the nearest band member and the music stops. She claps her hands and says loudly,

"If everyone could line up beside Arthur, it's time for the happy couple to leave us for their wedding night."

Finn looks at me in surprise and I shrug as the guests start to arrange themselves in a line as ordered to.

Finn wanders over and Sable laughs. "Your friends have been preparing a night to remember, I don't think you will be disappointed."

She winks and I feel the excitement build once again as I wonder what they've done.

"Ok, guys, say goodnight to your guests, it's home time."

As we make our way down the line, there are many happy tears as we say goodnight to our guests. It feels a little bitter sweet to be drawing the curtains on the happiest day of my life, but at least I know we have many tomorrows to look forward to. As we reach the end of the line, Sable and Arthur are standing there and say loudly, "Ok, everybody grab a lantern, it's dark but not far."

"Where are we going?" I whisper to Finn and he shrugs. "Who knows?"

We follow Sable and Arthur and the rest of the wedding party settle in behind us, as we start walking towards the lake. The moonlight reflects in the still water and lights up the shadows as we pass. I grip Finn's hand tightly as we form a strange procession as we weave our way through the trees that surround the lake with the castle reflected in the still crystal water.

About fifteen minutes later, we reach a small clearing and I gasp. My heart lifts as I see a little wooden cabin appear through the trees. It looks like a shepherd's hut and all around it are little fairy lights strung among the branches. Bunting is strewn along the front of it, spelling out our names and the smell of wood-smoke lingers in the air.

It looks like the most magical place on earth and Finn appears as astonished as I am, as Harvey says loudly, "Now you know why Heidi and I kept sneaking off."

I stare at them in amazement and Heidi grins with excitement. "Sable ordered the shepherd's hut to be delivered when you were both away from the castle, us at the spa and Harvey and Finn in town. When we returned, Harvey and I were instructed to make it fit for a king and his queen and we had to keep it a secret. Everybody had a hand in it though and inside is a little gift from everyone to make it special."

I stare in amazement and for once words fail me as the guests laugh and are obviously enjoying the surprise.

Then Sable claps her hand once more and says loudly, "Ok, let's leave the newlyweds to enjoy their first night as a married couple and we can catch up with them again in the morning."

One by one, the guests leave and soon it's just the two of us, standing in the clearing on the edge of the lake, faced with the most romantic night ahead a bride could ever wish for.

Taking my hand, Finn says huskily, "It reminds me of our first night together."

"What camping?"

"Yes, although it's a step up from a pop-up tent and a wheelie case."

I shrug. "It was perfect, to me, anyway, just like this is perfect and I wouldn't want to be anywhere else."

Suddenly, Finn sweeps me into his arms and growls, "Come on Mrs Roberts. I'm carrying you over the threshold because what happens next will not wait another minute."

As he kicks open the door to the little shepherd hut, I think I am the happiest I have ever been in my life.

Epilogue

One Year Later

"Happy Anniversary, darlin'."

I burst out laughing as Finn enters the room wearing nothing but an apron, carrying a tray full of breakfast things decorated with a small daisy in a vase.

"What's all this?"

"Just keeping the magic alive."

He grins as he sets the tray down on the bed and jumps in beside me.

"So, the calm before the storm."

I nod and lift a warm croissant to my lips and inhale the scent of a little piece of heaven.

"What time are they due?"

"I think we have an hour."

I groan and shake my head as he laughs. "Are you ready for round two?"

"I'm not so sure. I mean, we've had a lot of practice over the last year, but this one's special."

Finn pours us a coffee and I think about the chaos that is about to descend on us in one hours' time.

A knock on the door interrupts my thinking and Heidi says loudly, "Is the coast clear?"

Finn rolls his eyes as I say hastily. "Of course. Come in."

I smile as Heidi bounds into the room with Mark trailing behind her looking apologetic. "I'm sorry, sis, but you know what she's like, couldn't wait."

I look at her with excited curiosity as she places a huge white box tied with a pink satin bow on the bed between us and says quickly, "Open it, it won't wait."

Her excitement rubs off on me and as she takes the tray and places it on the bedside table, I pull the satin bow apart and Finn says, "What's that noise?"

"Open it!"

Heidi and Mark say in one voice and so we quickly open the box and gasp in surprise as a little head pops out, bringing tears to my eyes.

"Oh my god, a puppy, I can't believe it."

I look at Finn in astonishment. "Did you know about this?"

"No, I didn't."

Reaching into the box, he pulls out the most gorgeous ball of fur that is looking at us with large brown, soulful eyes and my heart fills with immediate love for the adorable puppy who is wagging its tail so hard, it thumps against the box as we rescue it from incarceration.

Heidi's eyes are shining as she says softly, "What are you going to call her?"

"I don't know?"

I stare at Finn and he laughs as he pats the little dog's head. "What about Daisy?"

"After my Aunt?" I stare at him in surprise and he nods. "Why not?"

As the little dog looks at me with curiosity, I laugh as she licks my hand and wags her tail, staring at me with eyes full of hope and adoration and I bury my face into her silken fur and feel the tears build as I whisper, "Daisy, what a perfect name for a perfect puppy."

She wriggles a little in my arms and I look up and say gratefully, "Thank you, she's perfect. I can't believe you bought us a puppy, it's the best present you could have ever given us."

Heidi smiles and takes Mark's hand and they stare at us, with happiness in their eyes. "It's the least we could do. You've given us so much and well, we owe you."

Seeing their happy faces is more than enough for me because the last year has panned out better than I dreamt possible. Mark and Heidi have settled into life at the Castle of Dreams and are responsible for the smooth running of a business that took off like a space ship to the moon. Our feet haven't touched the ground and we are always at maximum occupancy which has proven a testing time for us all. One year on and history is about to repeat itself because today another set of guests arrive and this time it's special.

Heidi looks at her watch and says briskly, "Anyway, we'll leave you to it because the guests will be arriving shortly. I'll take Daisy and settle her in while you get ready."

Reluctantly, I hand the wriggling puppy to Heidi and as they leave the room, Finn laughs softly.

"Why on earth did they think a puppy was a good idea, today of all days?"

"That's Heidi for you, act first, think later. I'm sure it will be fine though, after all, there will be quite a lot of us to keep the little one in check."

"Yes, it should be one to remember."

Leaning across, I make to grab the tray to finish what we started and Finn pulls me back and into his arms, saying huskily, "Not so fast."

As he kisses me softly and with a building passion, I sigh and think I'll never stop loving every minute of this. Yes, today is a special day alright because once again the Castle of Dreams is hosting a wedding. Over the next few days history will repeat itself and another couple will marry exactly one year on from when they first met. Yes, Finn will return the favour and be the best man to *his* best man. Harvey and Sybil are set to marry and I will be the matron of honour. Once again, Sable will swoop down on us in her helicopter with the happy couple and their families will arrive in a minibus. My own family are also on hand to help with the event which should make things easier but knowing them, will just add to the chaos.

At least we won't have to worry about Stella and Piers because by a miracle of nature, Piers woke up one day and realised his new life wasn't a patch on his old one and it was fun to watch Stella making it very difficult for him to win her back. However, after a Caribbean holiday and lots and lots of grovelling, he won fair lady and they are happier than they have ever been. Mum and Dad are as mad as ever and thankfully all sets of grandparents are in good health and just as crazy and long may it continue to be so.

After the longest kiss and with a great deal of reluctance, Finn pulls away and smiles. "Happy anniversary, Adams."

"I was going to say that, Roberts, why do you always get there first?"

We grin as a high-pitched bark can be heard from the garden outside and Finn rolls his eyes. "A puppy, god help us."

"Could be worse."

"Explain."

"Well, put it this way, this time next year it won't just be a puppy barking, in fact, I'm guessing leisurely breakfasts in bed will be a thing of the past for quite a while."

Suddenly, the penny drops and the look in Finn's eye makes me burst into tears as I nod and he smiles happily as he crushes me in his arms and says huskily, "Thank you."

"It takes two, you know."

Just for a moment we stop as the pages of the notebook turn again and a new chapter begins. The family tree is about to get another branch and life couldn't be better.

The End

Thank you for reading The Wedding at the Castle of Dreams.

If you liked it, I would love if you could leave me a <u>review</u>, as I must do all my own advertising.

This is the best way to encourage new readers and I appreciate every review I can get. Please also recommend it to your friends as word of mouth is the best form of advertising. It won't take longer than two minutes of your time, as you only need write one sentence if you want to.

Have you checked out my website? Subscribe to keep updated with any offers or new releases.

When you visit my website, you may be surprised because I don't just write Romantic comedy.

I also write under the pen names M J Hardy & Harper Adams. I send out a monthly newsletter with details of all my releases and any special offers but aside from that you don't hear from me very often.

I do however love to give you something in return for your interest which ranges from free printables to bonus content. If you like social media please follow me on mine where I am a lot more active and will always answer you if you reach out to me.

Why not take a look and see for yourself and read Lily's Lockdown, a little scene I wrote to remember the madness when the world stopped and took a deep breath.

sjcrabb.com

Lily's Lockdown
(Just scroll to the bottom of the page and click the link to read for free.)

If you want to know how Finn and Lily met check out

Aunt Daisy's Letter

More books by S J Crabb

The Diary of Madison Brown

My Perfect Life at Cornish Cottage

My Christmas Boyfriend

Jetsetters

More from Life

A Special Kind of Advent

Fooling in love

Will You

Holly Island

Aunt Daisy's Letter

The Wedding at the Castle of Dreams

sjcrabb.com

Printed in Great Britain
by Amazon

42836370R00159